MW01126981

CONVICTIONS OF THE HEART

CONVICTIONS OF THE HEART

KA Murray

iUniverse, Inc.
New York Bloomington

Convictions of the Heart

Copyright © 2008 by KA Murray

All rights reserved. No part of this book may be used or reproduced by any
means, graphic, electronic, or mechanical, including photocopying, recording,
taping or by any information storage retrieval system without the written
permission of the publisher except in the case of brief quotations embodied in
critical articles and reviews.

This is a work of fiction. All of the characters, names, incidents, organizations,
and dialogue in this novel are either the products of the author's imagination or
are used fictitiously.

iUniverse books may be ordered through booksellers or by contacting:

iUniverse
1663 Liberty Drive
Bloomington, IN 47403
www.iuniverse.com
1-800-Authors (1-800-288-4677)

Because of the dynamic nature of the Internet, any Web addresses or links
contained in this book may have changed since publication and may no longer be
valid. The views expressed in this work are solely those of the author and do not
necessarily reflect the views of the publisher, and the publisher hereby disclaims
any responsibility for them.

ISBN: 978-0-595-52333-7 (pbk)
ISBN: 978-0-595-51091-7 (cloth)
ISBN: 978-0-595-62389-1 (ebk)

Printed in the United States of America

ACKNOWLEDGEMENTS

I haven't been blessed with children as of yet, but completing this book has definitely been a labor of love. The fact that this book is now in print; it reaffirms my belief that all things are possible if you create a vision for yourself; have the dedication and determination to press forth even when you feel like giving up, and believe that God truly has a wonderful plan for your life if you just believe. As I begin a new phase in my life and as God continues to reveal his plan to me, I will continue to walk out on faith and onto a new path, although, I may not be sure of my ultimate destination, I do know that as long as I put God first in all that I do, he will light my course and order my steps.

I want to say thank you to everyone that has been instrumental and an inspiration to me as I struggled and toiled to complete this book. To my parents, all that I am is because of you and words could not express my gratitude for all that you have done for me. To Louis (a.k.a Pep) thank you for all of the memories. We've come a long way and I wouldn't change anything for the world. Everything that has occurred in our lives has shaped us into the people we are today and the best is yet to come. A special thank you goes out to my friends: Zilla, who was just a phone call away to encourage me when I doubted myself; Ms. Bea, who constantly reminded me that God hasn't forgotten me, and Linda, who made me laugh when I wanted to cry; you all will never know how I truly appreciated your support and words of wisdom.

It has been a long journey and God is the one constant that has never failed me and "because he lives I can face tomorrow, because he lives all fear is gone, because I know he holds the future, life is worth the living just because he lives." To anyone that has a dream, I encourage you to believe in yourself and press forward because I'm proof that dreams really do come true.

CHAPTER 1

It seems like a lifetime ago that I was married to Lance Weldon. When we met he was everything I thought I was looking for in a future husband: young, gifted, and black. When we met as undergrads at the University of Florida, Lance was my knight in shining armor. He was the star runner on the men's track and field team in his junior year while I was a sophomore on the women's. We were both highly recruited 400-meter runners so it was only natural for us to be placed together as training partners.

Our relationship began as friends, but I'll admit he was always my ebony prince, and I idolized everything about him. He stood 6'3" and was a lean 185 pounds with light brown eyes and lickable lips like LL Cool J. I would salivate during practice as I dreamed of his long legs entwined with mine as we made love.

This wasn't a one-way deal, I was equally eye-catching at 5'10" and 140 pounds with natural sandy brown hair and freckles sprinkled on my nose, compliments of my mother. I was also often complimented on my "junk in the trunk," as Jerome from the sitcom *Martin* was always teasing Pam about.

We were definitely a striking pair, even if I was the only one who thought so. Our relationship would never have evolved if it weren't for my persistence. I confess I was the one who pursued Lance. He was extremely nerdy, not to mention oblivious to the clumsy way I would bump into or trip over him as we practiced our starting blocks and sprint drills. He was serious business when it came to preparing for our track meets and conference title, so he wasn't swayed by my attempts to entice him.

Lance majored in Criminal Justice, which was my major as well, and he maintained a 4.0 GPA all while competing and traveling with the team. I was no slacker either when it came to my courses, I maintained a 3.5 GPA, and we both made the dean's list and shared the title of scholar athlete.

As focused as I was on receiving my degree, I was also determined to make Lance notice me. I knew Lance was the first one in his family to attend college. He was not going to be deterred by me, which is why he paid me no attention on or off the track. However, Lance had no idea as to what type of woman he was messing with. When it came to getting what I wanted, I wouldn't stop until I had him loving everything about me.

Everything was going smoothly until my coach decided he wanted me to move up to the 400-meter hurdles. I never particularly liked hurdles, it was hard enough to concentrate on running without any obstacles in my way, but I'd decided to try something new, and my coach assured me that it would build up my endurance for the 4x400 meter relay. In practice, I was running drills for my hurdle techniques. As I headed into the turn, my lead leg cleared the hurdle, but my trail leg got caught in it and I tumbled to the rubber track. I brushed it off, thinking about something my coach had told me earlier: "You're not a hurdler until you fall." But when I attempted to get up, my left leg buckled underneath me, and I immediately knew something was dreadfully wrong.

After I was carried to the training facility, the athletic trainer confirmed my suspicions and sent me off to the hospital. I'd torn my anterior cruciate ligament (the notorious ACL), and they scheduled me for knee surgery that week.

I was already infatuated with Lance, but I really fell head over heels for him when he came to cheer me up in the hospital after the surgery. He seemed to feel more horrible about the situation than I did. Lance held my hand and reassured me that before I knew it, we'd be on the track practicing like old times. But he was just trying to lift my spirits because I already knew I would be having a long recovery period. The doctor had told me I'd need a full year of rehabilitation before I even thought about stepping out on the track again. Shoot, running was the one thing I did best, and now I was being told my track season was over before I'd even been able to compete in the first track meet of the year.

I felt disappointed and discouraged about my athletic future, but I was surprised when my mom announced she would come up to Gainesville from Miami to assist me during my recuperating phase until I could manage on my own. Even my ex-boyfriend Carl had the nerve to show up at the hospital to see how I was doing. He and I had been broken up for some time, but we were finally on speaking terms with one another, and he said he'd come by the hospital just to make sure that I was alright, it was a nice gesture but I really didn't want to see him.

I was grateful for everyone who came by, but having Lance there was the cherry on top of my sundae. All it took for him to build up the nerve to talk to me was my tripping over a hurdle and landing in a hospital bed. While Lance was sitting at my bedside, I found out he was secretly smitten with me. He said he would have never had the courage to admit how he felt towards me, but seeing me in the hospital looking so depressed; he finally found a way to admit his feelings. Lance said he'd looked forward to practice every day just because I was there, but since I would be rehabbing my knee, he knew he wouldn't get the chance to see me that often, so he needed to tell me how he actually felt.

Lance didn't have to utter one word because I wasn't listening to anything that he was saying anyway. I was happy just looking at him all day long, but to actually hear him say he liked me as much as I was digging him—it was enough to make me forget my pain from surgery. I no longer had to find ways for him to notice me. Having him here with me meant the world to me and just the sight of him made me feel as if I were going to be just fine. If he saw me at my worst, then I could really count on him to be there through thick and thin.

CHAPTER 2

Lance and I became an official couple after my stay in the hospital, but my aspirations for running track were never the same after my knee surgery. Much of track and field is technique and timing. The spring in my step was completely off, and I just couldn't regain my timing because of the weight I'd gained during my year of rehabilitation. I was frustrated because I could no longer compete at a level that was better than when I arrived in Gainesville. Because I was on scholarship, I received a medical redshirt for the year I went through rehabilitation, and once I returned to the track, I was obligated to give my best efforts during practice and meets. However, I silently struggled with the feeling B. B. King so eloquently described: "The Thrill is Gone." I once had dreams of being in the Olympics and becoming a household name like Evelyn Ashford, or Marion Jones before she pleaded guilty because of her involvement in the steroid case with BALCO.

The only thing that I could count on and that was a constant in my life was Lance. By this time, Lance had graduated and I was in my senior year. We moved into a condo together, and he was lucky enough to find a job in the area. Because of his good grades and his internship over the summer, Lance was quickly hired on as a federal probation officer for the Department of Justice. This was a job many people coveted, and Lance became an office favorite because of his hard work, commitment to his duties, and determination to do a good job. I was so proud of him and all of his accomplishments, and I also knew he would succeed at anything he put his mind to.

While Lance was finding his way professionally, I was still struggling with what I really wanted to do once I graduated. I truly loved the criminal justice field. It afforded me countless opportunities from which to choose an exciting career, but I just didn't know where to begin.

Just before I was scheduled to graduate, I was still stressed about what direction I wanted to pursue professionally. I didn't want to leech off of Lance—I wanted to be a contributor in this relationship. After all, we weren't married, and I couldn't expect him to be the sole provider. He was already sending his mother money when he could afford to, and I just didn't feel right burdening him by making him take me on as an added problem.

Graduation was only a few months away and I was consumed with the idea of finding suitable employment. Just when I thought all hope was lost, I attended a job fair on campus and found what I was looking for. I'd stopped at a table for the Federal Bureau of Prisons whose recruiter spoke to me about the endless number of opportunities for advancement within the agency. I was intrigued from his first words. If I applied for a job with the BOP, which was also a branch of the Department of Justice, my promotional potential would increase. If I were willing to relocate, I could quickly rise up the professional ladder. I had no reservations as I filled out an application and determined my preferred states where I was interested in working. Things were looking up for me, and I couldn't wait to tell Lance about my decision.

However, I knew Lance had become use to me depending on him to make all of the crucial decisions about how our relationship would evolve. Now I was afraid he couldn't grasp the notion that I was taking charge and making a concrete decision about what I wanted to do. Applying for a job with the BOP made me feel good, I felt as if I were finally focused on the future. I knew I was walking into that future with a well-organized plan. When I informed Lance about what happened at the job fair and explained how excited I was to find something that piqued my interest on so many levels, true to form he understood and indicated he would support me with whatever decision I made.

I was lucky to have a man like Lance in my life. Where I got anxious and worried about everything, he was rational and calm. Those were some of the things opposite of my own traits that attracted me to this man, and I didn't know what I would do if he wasn't in my life to create a sense of balance. I was uncertain how the next few months would change our lives, but I was sure I didn't want to lose Lance—he was my heart.

CHAPTER 3

It was hard to believe that four years could come and go so fast. I've had my share of ups and downs, but now I was celebrating my graduation day with my wonderful boyfriend and my parents and sisters who all made the drive from Miami. The best part of the day was that I'd accepted a job offer to become a correctional officer in downtown Miami at the Federal Detention Center. I was excited but a little leery about having a long-distance relationship, so I was planning for Lance and me to have an in-depth discussion during my celebration dinner to see if our love for one another could withstand the separation.

Because my family wanted to return to Miami after the graduation ceremony (as usual my mom was in a hurry to get back to her empty house), Lance and I decided to continue the celebration back at our condo. Instead of taking me out to dinner, Lance prepared a home-cooked meal of a garden salad, chicken fettuccine with Alfredo sauce, and garlic bread.

Lance cooking dinner was fantastic as well as a complete surprise. I would have made him cook more often if I'd known he could throw down like this. He capped off the night with a delicious chocolate cake which I recognized as my mom's recipe, and we toasted with champagne our hopes for a good future and our promise to remain faithful to one another.

It was at this moment that I noticed something foreign swimming in the bottom of my champagne glass, and I turned to see Lance down on one knee. He looked at me so lovingly with tears in his eyes as he said, "Denise, you are my best friend, and I couldn't think of living in this world without you by my side. Would you please do me the honor of becoming my wife?" I had no idea that this proposal was coming, and I was completely dazed by the question. When Lance asked, "What's your answer, Denise?" I accepted his offer without hesitation, and we melted into each other's arms and kissed for what seemed like an eternity.

Reality hit me while we embraced, and I asked Lance what my new job offer would mean to us. He said, "Oh, don't worry about it—my other surprise is that I've accepted a job promotion as the chief federal probation officer in Fort Lauderdale."

That night I gave Lance a sample of how our lovemaking would be after we became husband and wife. First, I escorted him to the bedroom and removed all of his clothing. I massaged him from the crown of his head to the bottom of his feet as he moaned and groaned at my sensual touches. As I mounted him, I was ready for him to feel just how he made my insides melt with the anticipation of feeling his love muscle pulsating deep inside of me. I rode Lance like a skilled equestrian until he exploded inside of me, cementing our undying love for one another. I felt my entire body tremble from the burst of hot fluid that released into me. After two more rounds of making love, I collapsed on his chest, and we fell asleep wrapped up in the rapture of our passion.

CHAPTER 4

Lance and I didn't have an elaborate wedding. Between trying to sell Lance's condo, packing up all of our personal items, and finding a home in South Florida, we didn't have the time, much less the funds, to waste on a big wedding. Instead we exchanged vows at the Broward County Courthouse. It was nothing spectacular, but I was just happy to finally be Mrs. Lance Weldon.

The major business at hand was to find a residence that would be convenient for me to commute to downtown Miami, yet close enough for him to drive to Ft. Lauderdale. It made more sense to me for us to spend our money on the closing costs of a home than to be in debt for the next five years for a wedding that neither we nor our families could afford.

With what Lance made from the sale of his condo and a hefty donation as a wedding gift from my parents, we were able to put a sizeable down payment on a home in Pembroke Pines. It seemed we'd decided to buy a home at the right moment. We found our home through foreclosure listings, and the bank was willing to negotiate with us; we paid less than half for a home valued at $250K.

Our starter purchase was a three bedroom, with two bathrooms, screened-in patio, and single car garage. I found it easy to persuade Lance to go along with selecting this house; he didn't have any complaints just as long as I was happy. I was head over heels about the house we'd chosen, with a little paint and decorating, we would make it the perfect home.

But I felt like everything was happening so fast. In just a matter of months, I'd gotten married, purchased a new home, and started preparing for my new job. I was dizzy from the excitement of it all.

We had so much to do and so little time to do it in. We both had reporting dates for our new jobs, all we had was a week to get unpacked and organize our new home. My sisters, Deborah and Diane, were glad I was back in the area, and I was happy we could hang out together again.

Once Lance and I got settled in our new home, I got reacquainted with my hometown. I was happy about returning to Miami. My parents lived in Miami Lakes, which was close enough for me to visit frequently if I missed them, yet far enough that they would have to think twice about just popping over.

Now my parents, who are Jonas and JoAnn Martin to everyone else but Pops and Mom to me, have been married for twenty-eight years. I find them hilarious—every time I see them, it's like watching some kind of comedy show. She constantly nags him, so he's always pretending he doesn't hear a word that she says. I know just how Pops feels, I also try my best to ignore Mom when she starts running her mouth. That's how it's been all of my life, and they are too old to change now, so I have to love them just they way they are. When it comes to setting an example, I think all kids single out something that their parents did or didn't do, and they make a vow to themselves that they will "never" repeat the actions of their parents. God knows I've said it a million times: I will not become JoAnn Martin.

I'm not saying that my folks are all bad, but you have to factor in how people grew up in order to understand why they behave the way they do when they become adults. I didn't have any children yet so I didn't know exactly how difficult it was to raise them, but I think my parents could have been more active in the lives of my sisters and me. I say that because I've participated in sporting events for the majority of my life, yet I can count the number of times my parents attended one of my track meets on one hand—and that's minus two fingers. Shoot, I would have loved to look up in the stands and see them cheering me on, but Pops was always working or Mom had a prior commitment to some church group she was in charge of. I guess they figured as long as my sisters and me were clothed and fed that was enough to show us they loved us. I felt that when I was fortunate enough to have kids, they'd probably have something to say about how I raised them, but I was going to make sure I showed up for every event because nothing would ever take precedence over my children. They might accuse me of smothering them to death, but at least they would know they were loved.

Even though I felt neglected at times, I think I turned out just fine. No one has a perfect childhood, and to hear my parents talk about their lives, I know things weren't easy for them either. Mom was an only child, and as with many children in the South growing up in the early 1940s, she was raised by her paternal grandparents. Her mother left her when she was two years old, and while she was growing up, her dad was in and out of her life. He was on the road trying to find stable work, something that would allow him to send some money home to help support her. She told us how she felt out of place in her grandmother's home where as the eldest grandchild; she grew up with many of her aunts and uncles.

Although she hated the idea of being in the fields, she had to work the farm when she came home from school. To get out of farm work, my mom learned how to cook really well so preparing dinner became her chore instead of the hard labor of tending to the farm.

Despite feeling out of place, my mom excelled in school, which she knew early on was her sure bet for making it out of the Georgia woods. She did just that after high school, she packed up her few belongings and left her grandmother's home without looking back. She caught a bus to Miami and found a job in a local restaurant where she worked every evening while attending nursing school during the day. She was able to get by on the little bit of money her father saved for her over the years. It took her seven long years to graduate, but eventually she prevailed.

This is the story that I'd heard over and over while I was growing up. It got so bad that when she started to tell it, my sisters and me would finish it for her. Mom told us, "Mock me if you want to, but I'm a living witness that you can do anything that you put your mind to. As long as you trust and believe in God, he will see you through anything." We knew she meant well, but she wouldn't let us forget that as she didn't have an easy life, she thought we should focus on what's important rather than wasting our time on trivial things.

I don't know which one of us she thought was wasting time. If anything, she should have been talking to Diane, who thought she could get away with murder just because she had a pretty face and a big ass. As for Deborah and me, I'd like to think we listened to the majority of what Mom was always nagging us about, but once we became adults, I thought it was unnecessary for her to constantly remind us of what she was doing when she was our age or tell us how we should be living our lives.

Now Pops—he's a whole different story. He was also raised by his paternal grandparents, but he left home when he was only sixteen. He obtained employment with the railroad system, which allowed him to travel and meet and greet people all over the countryside. Through his travels, he saw the world, even if it was sometimes the unsavory side. I can remember him telling us all about how black people weren't allowed to sit in the same travel cars with white people, and how he had to serve white people who didn't even want to sit next to him. He grew up when segregation was the norm, and as a black man coming into his own, he experienced discrimination, yet it didn't make him bitter. He believed that it's just how people were back in those days, and through the blood, sweat, and tears of civil rights leaders; things have changed drastically for the better for black people.

He's preached to me and my sisters as well, and he always instilled in us that life isn't easy, but that we have to get up every day and face whatever challenges may come, that we should believe we can do anything with the Lord guiding us, and that we should never take no for an answer. Pops could get real deep sometimes, but he'd seen a lot and he was just trying to expose us to the harsh realities of this world. However, he didn't do it all the time like my mom—he's cool, and he's always been real easy to talk to. Maybe he's just been pretending not to listen which is why he can ignore my mom so well.

After his rambling days with the railroad, my dad decided to settle down, and he soon met and married my mother in Miami. After just three years of marriage, they had my older sister, Deborah, then me, and my baby sister Diane followed soon after. My sisters and I are only two years apart in age so we enjoyed and supported one another as we were growing up. Actually we had no other choice since my parents were always busy doing something else.

After working for the railroad system for forty years, Pops retired, but Mom still worked part-time in the hospital as a nurse, and when she wasn't at the hospital, she helped out in the church. If I were retired with three grown daughters, I would be traveling all over the world, but not my folks, they don't do much traveling. I guess my dad got all of his traveling out of his system while he was with the railroad company. That's why he's content just hanging around the house, landscaping, and being a deacon in the church. As for my mom, she's afraid to leave the house for any extended period of time, for some strange reason she believes that if she's not there to protect the home, someone will just come and steal the entire thing. I don't know what she thinks the homeowner's insurance she pays for is supposed to do.

CHAPTER 5

After we settled in, everything in my life was great for the moment, and I thanked God for all of the blessings I'd been experiencing: I had a handsome new husband and exciting new job, and I was back home with my family. Everything was just as it should be.

Before my orientation began with the Bureau of Prisons, I had to learn several alternate routes to work. I traveled during rush hour traffic just to gauge the actual time I should allow for getting there on time. On my first day, I was a little apprehensive about what to actually expect from my co-workers, and especially the inmates. But before I was released into the housing units alone, I first had to complete a two-week orientation course, and then go to basic training for three weeks at the Federal Law Enforcement Training Center (FLETC) in Brunswick, Georgia. I was anxious to participate with other new employees in role playing and developing scenarios in a prison-like setting.

The training process was actually fun for me. I had time to rest and determine if this was what I actually wanted for my professional career. One major bonus about the job was the salary, not too many businesses were paying what I was receiving straight out of college. I saw my new job as a means to an end, but I also liked that the possibilities for advancement were unlimited.

Since we were still newlyweds, Lance would come up to Brunswick on the weekends and we would make the best of our time together. We took mini-honeymoons, visiting the historical St. Simons Island. I enjoyed our walks along the pier and the beach. Lance and I even took this opportunity to do something a little freaky, by making love on the beach under the moonlight.

Our lovemaking got better each time around. When we first hooked up, Lance wasn't really experienced; however, just like wine improves with time, through meticulous guidance and instructions from me, his quality improved and I found him simply delicious. I loved the way that he took his time with me and looked at me so intently as if he were seeing me for the very first time, like he doesn't want to miss anything. He was so conscious of doing what it took to satisfy me, and I responded with moans and vibrations to let him know that he had all of me: mind, body, and soul.

The only thing bad about Lance's visits while I was in training was that they were over too quickly, but while I was in class all week long, it gave me something to look forward to for the weekend as well as an opportunity to daydream. After the first week, I had more than my share of self-defense and firearms training. While we were at the gun range for three hours of the day, it was scorching hot, with the temperature sometimes reaching 110 degrees. I thought to myself, *if hell is this hot, then I have to do everything in my power not to go there.*

Three weeks was a long time for me to be away from my husband, so graduation day at FLETC couldn't come soon enough for me. I became an Honor Graduate for receiving the highest test scores in my class. Once I received my plaque, certificate of completion, and class photo, I was on I-95 South, ready to see my man and rest in my own bed before I had to report to work on Monday morning.

CHAPTER 6

The Federal Detention Center (FDC) sure did not look like any prison that I had ever seen on television. You could have mistaken it for any other high-rise office in downtown Miami, but once you passed the front lobby and took the elevator to the inmate housing units, the sight of inmates and cells let you know this was a high-level security facility. It housed some of South Florida's most notorious and powerful criminals, such as members of the Zo Pound Gang, the Boobie Boys, Gambino Crime Family, and Vonda's Gang. The majority of the inmates were awaiting trial for their criminal charges, they were known as pre-trial inmates; while others were awaiting transfer to their designated facilities because they had either been found guilty of a crime, or they had accepted a plea agreement instead of taking their chances with a jury trial and these inmates were known as holdovers. It was alarming for me on my first day at work to see over 1200 inmates within the facility waiting to learn their fate, and ultimately serve out their time in federal prisons throughout the country. I don't care what anyone says about basic training or how many episodes of the television show *Oz* on HBO I watched, nothing prepared me for being trapped in a housing unit with over one hundred convicts with my only means of alerting anyone of danger being via a handheld radio or telephone.

Being a correctional officer is much like being a high priced babysitter. According to my job description, my primary duties were to maintain the care, custody, and control of inmates; in actuality I was a mediator settling disputes between inmates before they escalated into a vicious fight over something as trivial as breakfast cereal. (The inmates craved the sugar-coated ones, particularly Frosted Flakes, which were the most coveted breakfast item.) My responsibilities also included alerting my supervisors to any strange or unusual behaviors exhibited by an inmate or a particular disruptive group. The highlight of my profession, which they neglected to advise us about in basic training, was also being responsible for dispensing toiletry items as well as being the source of information when an inmate had an issue with one of the various departments within the institution.

Some days I felt more burdened than others, especially with the inmates who had done a considerable amount of time in the federal system and thus became extremely knowledgeable about the rules and regulations of the BOP. They wanted to be granted every privilege they were entitled to receive from the U.S. government while they were in custody. Often, these inmates abused medical and dental services, complained about the food, and watched every move the employees made just in case someone did something not in accordance with policy or procedure. This then gave them an opportunity to file a frivolous lawsuit to overload an already congested legal system and put taxpayer dollars to work on behalf of those who got their thrills from making the lives of correctional workers miserable.

Don't get me wrong now: the job that I do isn't for everyone, and it can get downright tedious at times (and I think if the inmates wanted all of the comforts of home, then they should have kept out of trouble and stayed there), but there are also those moments when I get to witness the dynamics of human behavior, and that makes my job worthwhile. I get to interact with and observe different cultures trying to coexist in an atmosphere that is stressful, due in part to the fact that inmates housed in penal facilities are trying to fight for their freedom, maintain a relationship with significant others from a distance, and contend with the pressures they face while attempting to adjust to new living arrangements that lacks any privacy. When you compound all of these elements of "doing time," it makes you wonder why anyone would want to become a career criminal. But there are some individuals who just can't function as law-abiding citizens, and prison is the environment in which they choose to thrive and define their purpose for living. For true convicts, the main objective while they are doing time is to get away with as much as possible without bringing too much attention to their unauthorized practices.

The prison system operates just like society, even behind bars inmates have to survive, and they do so by hustling, which includes selling drugs they've smuggled into the institution through visitation or other means, being a personal cook for some of the more financially stable inmates, gambling, or becoming a sex toy for the inmates that prefer men. For repeat offenders or those with lengthy prison sentences, being a career criminal may have its just rewards.

However, in addition to hardened criminals, we had inmates who have been convicted only of some minor felony crime. Their sentence generally ranged from five months to one year and a day, which made no sense to me, especially considering just how much it costs to house and care for an inmate. Why would you send someone to jail for just a few months? Instead, I would place them on house arrest or give them a hefty fine, especially since most people tend to respond when you hit them where it hurts—in the pocket! Those with short sentences usually just want to do their time without getting caught up in the games the other convicts play.

One of the most amusing things I have witnessed while working in a correctional setting was the inmates who become jailhouse lawyers. These are the ones who feel as if they've been railroaded by the system, often due in part to overworked public defenders who couldn't prepare adequately for their trial, so they usually received the maximum penalty. Now they felt it was up to them to find a loophole in the laws that could ultimately change the length of their stay at "Club Fed." They also offered their services to other inmates who claimed to have been unjustly convicted of crime. What I found almost comical was that some of them could have actually been very good attorneys had they made different choices in life.

Some inmates don't fall into either of those categories. A few have been transformed by the renewing of their hearts and souls. These are the ones who are now saved, sanctified, and filled with the Holy Spirit. Being in prison affords many inmates the opportunity to find again something they hadn't really lost. They truly believe Jesus, Allah, Buddha, or some other higher power has finally come into their lives so that they will be forgiven for all their sins and start anew upon rejoining society. This can be a way of life for them 24 hours, 7 days a week because they had to pass the time some kind of way.

The most annoying thing for me as an officer was when inmates thought they had all the common sense in the world, so they tried to enlighten me as to how I'd become a pawn for "the man" and how working for the "feds" had somehow brainwashed me into keeping the brothas down. I got so sick of inmates thinking they knew so much more than free people. When I got fed up with their trying to explain to me the error of my ways, I asked: "If you had so much sense, then how in the world were you dumb enough to let the feds catch you?" That response usually embarrassed them and sent them on their way until they were brave enough to ask me some other silly question.

I can tolerate just about anything, especially if it means that it will lead to something more promising and prosperous. Dealing with so many individuals with various personal issues is overwhelming at first, but when you've been in the law enforcement field for a while, it's easy to become desensitized even at times when I should have been compassionate towards others. I also became a little more skeptical about what ulterior motives others may have when I dealt with them on a personal basis.

CHAPTER 7

I found having such an unusual job and being a newlywed could be quite stressful, but my husband also had a career in law enforcement as a chief probation officer, and I never had to explain when I'd had a bad day. I understood his position as well, and being the "Top Cop" in the probation office meant his duties included supervising other probation officers and reviewing the reports they submitted to the U.S. District Courts, the U.S. Parole Commission, and the federal prison system regarding the background and activities of people either charged with or having been found guilty of federal offenses. Because our jobs encompassed a variety of stressors, Lance fully understood the daily rigors of mine, and I didn't have to explain why my feet and back were killing me from standing and walking around a housing unit all day long trying to keep the peace between confused, scared, or know-it-all inmates. I also understood how accountability was a major factor in his job. If his probation officers weren't conducting interviews or checking to see if inmates are adhering to the guidelines of their release, it reflected back on Lance and his ability to supervise others.

I usually didn't have to utter a word and Lance could tell by the expression on my face when I walked in the front door what kind of day I've had. He would dutifully run water for my bath and begin dinner. Oh, how I loved that man of mine. It was just the little things he did that made my heart flutter. I always told him, it's the doing without the asking that I truly appreciated. When my man was so thoughtful towards me, I couldn't help but to reward him with mind-blowing sex. I enjoyed the fact that it was just the two of us, and we had a chance to escape within ourselves and exist as if we were the only people on the planet. He loved me so tenderly and I automatically responded to his touches and kisses. As the old Calgon commercials contended, he just took me away from whatever problems I had before I arrived home. When I made love to Lance, I fell in love with him all over again. We'd grown together, and now that our careers were starting to take off, we were definitely living the American Dream. I couldn't help but think that things could only get better between us.

Lance and I are still young and vibrant; we learned early on what most couples usually figure out in the latter part of their marriage: to keep the romance flowing, you definitely have to make time for each other. Despite what was going on with our families or our jobs, we always made time for a date night. It was just one day out of the week in which we concentrated on one another and made the night special. That didn't mean we had to do something extravagant— just take the time to learn more about ourselves and how we could grow as a couple. Our date night might include anything. Sometimes we rented a movie, turned off the telephone ringer, and just snuggled up with one another. Or we might go out to dinner and enjoy a night at the movies. Plus because we were so young, we still enjoyed going out and getting our groove on every once in a while.

I don't particularly like the nightclub scene, but if Lance wanted to unwind by dancing or having a few drinks, I didn't think that was such a bad compromise to make my mate happy. We liked to go to the hotel El Palacio in Miami, which had a ballroom that usually turned into a nightclub on the weekends. It was a place where young adults went to mingle and network.

Being with my man meant that I didn't have to worry about anyone trying to make any moves on me; all I had to do was flash my two-carat diamond wedding ring, and they usually got the hint that I was already spoken for. But for some reason, women had the opposite reaction to Lance. I caught them on the floor giving him "the eye" while I was dancing with him. When I noticed someone trying to entice my man and disrespect me on the sly, I strategically, methodically and seductively danced for my husband, which provoked him to literally "stand at attention" so everyone could see who had his heart. I can do a booty dance that would put Ms. Ciara, the new Queen of Crunk, to shame, which halted any vultures who thought they might have a chance of getting Lance's attention away from me.

The one special thing about our date night was that it always ended with the most magnificent, earth-shattering sex I could ever imagine. Lance was so gentle with me, and he knew how to make me feel good. He knew how I like to be kissed on my forehead and how I loved for him to gently work his way down to my red-light district, place his head between my thighs, and do things with his tongue that made me cringe with insane pleasure. Oh and trust me, I returned the favor in the same way—I could make him say my name and plead for me to stop because he just couldn't take anymore. I know that I had Lance because he couldn't even wait until I returned from the bathroom with a warm washcloth to wipe him off before I heard his soft snores. I just couldn't help but to laugh to myself and think *I have this man wrapped around my little finger.*

CHAPTER 8

After I graduated from college and moved back home, my mom started having these family dinners on Sunday evenings after church. Usually, my older sister would come with her husband, Kevin and their children, and my baby sister would bring her significant other (who changed with each family function), but as my work schedule was subject to change without notice, I wasn't available to attend regularly. If I couldn't make it to my folks' gatherings, Lance would make an appearance for the both of us, especially since it was in his best interest if he wanted something to eat because I wasn't going to come home from work on a Sunday and prepare an elaborate meal for him. When he did visit my parents, he always prepared a plate to go for me. Trust me when I say that I wasn't missing out anything by not attending those dinners.

I love my two sisters dearly, but with Deborah and Diane there is never a dull moment, and I sometimes wonder if they were secretly adopted. My older sister Deborah is a drama queen to say the least; she thinks everyone owes her something because she believes she had to give up on all the things she wanted to do because she was responsible for taking care of Diane and me. Now she was only two years older than me, and I definitely don't recall her having to do anything backbreaking when it came to me or my little sister. Deborah has a selective memory when it comes to our childhood experiences. Mom signed her up for cheerleading, basketball, volleyball, and any other sport or activity in which she was interested. It was Deb who lost enthusiasm the first moment she began to sweat from participation, and then she would declare she was suffering from an incurable disease so she could no longer engage in any activities. Because Deborah was not athletically inclined and Mom didn't want her to have an idle mind, she delegated Deborah to being responsible for making sure we got home safely from school and started our homework. Deb was also in charge of doing our hair, which was the one thing she was very good at. It was evident that Deborah found her calling early in life, she had the ability to transform the most untamed manes and make someone's head look like a work of art.

However, Deborah will tell anyone with ears that she raised my sister and me, swearing it was her punishment for being the eldest. For the life of me,

I don't know why anyone who complains as much as she does about raising children was simple enough in her senior year of high school to get pregnant by the star football player and give birth to not one, but two of the cutest little boys I ever laid my eyes on. Keith and Kelby, my twin nephews, were born nine months after Deborah graduated from high school, and they forced her to redirect her attention off of herself and devote more time to being a good mother. She married their father, Kevin, and despite the horrible statistics regarding the outcome of teenage pregnancy, they've done real well together.

While in high school, Deb had made extra cash by doing all the neighborhood girls' hair. You name it, she could create it—matter of fact, all she had to do was see a particular style in a magazine and she could not only duplicate it, but make it look better than the original. Pops believed in her talents so much that he borrowed against his retirement savings to buy Deborah a hair salon once she graduated from cosmetology school. The thing with Deb is that she's good and she knows it. Once she got her license and hired other beauticians that were good (but not as good as her), she was able to pay my dad back with interest within two years.

During this time, Deb's *Doo Right Hair Salon* was quite popular in the North Miami Beach area. Her appointment book was always full and clients had to call three weeks in advance for an appointment. I couldn't be one of her customers though, Deb knew women would pay top dollar for her skills, she didn't mind overbooking her clients and making them sit in the salon all damn day long waiting on her. But, I couldn't deny the end results were well worth the wait, I guess that's why her business was booming.

Now my baby sister, Diane, is too much for me as well. I think my mom must have dropped her on her head as a child because she doesn't have any common sense whatsoever. Because she's the baby in the family and everyone caters to her every need, she's pretty much spoiled rotten to this day. Being spoiled is all well and good when you're describing a child, but when you're a grown-ass woman, it's not so cute. I have no one to blame except my parents for the way she turned out. Right now she was in her last year of college— Lord help her when she had to get out in the real world.

Diane is very beautiful; she's tall, with full breasts and nice hips. She didn't get the boy body like me or Deb's 5'6" frame. Since Deb was responsible for our hair while growing up and she did a hell of a job, Diane is blessed with long, jet black hair that's always on point because of her regular salon visits to Deb's shop. Diane leaves Deb's shop looking like a beauty pageant contestant, but she never pays for the services; in fact she says that she should be paid for her advertisement of Deb's artwork since it will increase Deb's clientele. I'd really like to thump that girl upside her head just so she would get a clue that the world does not revolve around her.

With me being the middle child, you would think I would have been the one to seek more attention from my parents. I was the ugly duckling well into my late teens, and there certainly weren't any perks that came along with being the middle child. With all of Deborah's dramatics, I don't remember her being the one going to school looking like Bozo the clown. She also didn't have to wear hand-me-down clothes. Deb was short and pudgy while I was tall and skinny—I was wearing Capri pants before they were even in style at my school. Unlike Diane, I wasn't the baby, so I couldn't just cry and throw a temper tantrum to get what I wanted. If I tried some of the things Diane got away with, I would've gotten my butt beat.

To escape from my family even if only for a short time, I indulged myself in sports. Track and field turned out to be the perfect thing for me; it transformed my body from looking like Olive Oil to a striking swan. I have well-defined muscles in my thighs and a tight butt that any man would break his neck to take a second glance at. Because of track and field, I was able to run away from my troubles and straight towards a full scholarship at the University of Florida as one of the top female sprinters who ever came out of Miami-Dade County.

CHAPTER 9

I moved up quite rapidly within the Bureau of Prisons system, and within three years I was able to apply for the top Correctional Officer position which is a Senior Officer Specialist. I was able to rise through the ranks so rapidly due in part to my willingness to ask questions and take notes from experienced officers. Usually seasoned officers are reluctant to share any information with rookies; they let them research policies and procedures on their own, or just learn the hard way. I think the real reason my co-workers were so willing to share their knowledge with me was that the more that they showed me, the less amount of work they had to do. When it came to completing a task, I was no nonsense; I was strictly all about business, and I didn't tolerate too much silliness from co-workers or inmates.

Because I took great pride in being a reliable employee, my supervisors rewarded me for my strong work ethics, I was voted Officer of the Year and received Special Act Awards for my superior performance while completing my duties. However, when I received so many accolades, I found out who my true friends were. This was my first real job, and I never would have thought that I would have to deal with the kind backstabbing and jealousy that I now experienced in a government workplace, where I thought civilized professionals could coexist. Instead of my fellow workers being supportive of my efforts, I received anonymous letters in my staff mailbox suggesting I must be sleeping with a lieutenant or I was receiving preferential treatment just because I had a tight ass and pretty face. But the haters could say what they wanted to: I had a plan to succeed, and I wasn't going to let anyone deter me from my goals.

One thing that bugged me about the cowards who left nasty notes in my mailbox was that working in a correctional setting requires all employees to rely on one another. In case of an emergency, the people I worked with would be the ones to respond. It's vital in this type of setting that all workers respect and appreciate one another because the one person that despises me the most would probably be the one who would need a helping hand during an emergency. Besides, how could someone dislike me or have something negative to say about me without actually knowing what kind of individual I was? If having a no-nonsense attitude and being firm with inmates garnered me the reputation of being a bitch, I'd gladly accept the title.

I did have two girlfriends at work who I could confide in. Sabrina and Kristy were my mentors who steered me in the right direction and helped me to deflect the negativity of those who didn't want me to succeed. I could count on their advice about any workplace issues, and whenever I had a question about my duties or responsibilities, they showed me how to find policy directives.

Of course I wasn't oblivious to the typical workplace issues that are prevalent in most government agencies. We had office romances, Equal Employment Opportunity complaints, and ongoing internal issues resulting in grievances being filed by the local union office or the Special Investigative Services conducting investigations based on inmate snitches regarding staff members believed to be corrupt. I was able to stay away from all of the workplace drama because I had a life outside of work. I wasn't interested in who had left his wife for a co-worker and now the soon-to-be ex-wife was stalking the couple, or who was rumored to be having a relationship with an inmate. Getting caught up in any scandal that would make it into the *Miami Herald* wasn't part of my agenda. I wasn't antisocial—I just didn't associate with many people I worked with, and I was cool with that. Besides, the few times I did attend a company function, someone always drank a little too much and made a complete ass out of himself. After I was accosted at a company party, I had a valid reason to boycott all employee gatherings.

The first Christmas party I attended, a fellow officer whom I barely knew started doing pelvic thrusts on me while I was dancing with my husband. Not only was I mortified, but Lance was burning mad. He wasn't interested in hearing about anyone simply having too much to drink—he was ready to fight. I quickly ran off the dance floor with him and we went straight home. The following week at work, the officer who had gyrated against me wrote me an apology note and swore he didn't mean to offend me or my husband; he said he could barely recall the Christmas party at all. I was cool with his apology, but I promised myself I would never attend another employee function as long as I was employed with the BOP.

CHAPTER 10

Lance and I had been living the good life; we were enjoying our careers and loving each other. We were so busy working and saving our money that before we knew it, we had been going nonstop for almost five years without ever having a real vacation. I couldn't get the same dates as my husband because of my seniority status as a correctional officer. I was low on the totem pole and, I had to select from the dates that were available after the senior staff made their selections.

When my vacation rolled around, Lance was so busy with trying to hire new staff that he encouraged me to go and visit my best girlfriend from college. I hadn't seen Zondra in a while, I decided to use one of my weeks to hang out with her. Zondra Hill was my teammate on the track team, and we were roommates during our freshman and sophomore years in college. After undergraduate school, she went to the University of Georgia Law School, and she now worked as an entertainment lawyer at a firm in Atlanta. There she'd been kept busy negotiating the contracts of some of Atlanta's hottest entertainers and athletes. Some of her clients included players from the Atlanta Falcons and Atlanta Hawks, and she also represented a few artists off of Sean P. Diddy's new Bad Boy South record label. I was proud of her because she'd accomplished so much, all while raising her little brother and sister after her parents died in a car accident during our junior year of college. Even though I'd never told her, Zondra was my role model. Even with all that she'd been through, she still had a sense of humor, and I think she would have made a fortune as a comedienne. The one thing I truly loved her for was that she always gave me good, sound advice whether I liked what she said or not.

We're the same age and Zondra's wisdom and strength amazed me, but I guess when you have to raise two teenagers, you don't have too many choices except to grow up fast. Zondra had some help from her aunts when she needed a break from her siblings while they were in school and she was trying to maintain her scholarship, but she was the one who nursed them back to health when they were sick. She also attended their school extracurricular activities when we weren't traveling with the track team, she helped them with their homework, and disciplined them when they did something wrong. Now that they were grown, responsible, and gainfully employed citizens, Zondra knew she had done the right things even when she doubted herself.

When I announced I was coming to see her, Zondra said, "Hell, yeah," and she quickly got busy planning our week of pampering and fun. Once my plane landed in Atlanta, I retrieved my luggage from baggage claim. I'd told Zondra to just circle the airport until I came out, because ever since 9/11, getting in and out of any an airport is hell.

Zondra picked me up in her new Mercedes Benz SUV. I screamed and hugged my crazy friend who hadn't changed one bit in five years. Zondra was a sprinter on our track team, but at first glance you wouldn't think so. She's 5'5" and solid, not fat or chunky, her weight was evenly distributed on her body. In college we'd tease her by saying she reminded us of Gail Devers, one of the best United States 110-meter hurdlers to have ever graced a track. Just looking at her made it clear she could still give these young girls a run for their money. Zondra's specialty in college was the 100 and 200 meters, and when she competed, she was like a bullet. Zondra has shoulder-length curly hair, compliments of her Native American mother and her African American father. She also had the biggest hazel eyes that could mesmerize any man when she was working her mojo.

As she drove through downtown, we giggled like young girls and talked about people we'd gone to school with and what we'd each heard about how their lives were going. We also talked about my marriage and why she couldn't find a decent man. Zondra swore that all of the men in Atlanta had a mouth full of gold teeth (which causes bad breath), were "in the closet," or preferred white women. I tried to tell her that she was looking in the wrong places because she can't go to a nightclub, proceed to get drunk, and then think the man she takes home that night will be Mr. Right. Besides, if she's interested in someone and they go out on a few dates, she finds some kind of flaw in the man's finances or features that suddenly churns her stomach so she can no longer pretend to be interested in him. When breaking up with a boyfriend, Zondra always uses her job as an excuse, but the truth is, she really doesn't want to commit to a relationship.

My opinion about Zondra's personal life is that she is so intelligent that it intimidates most men, so she always seems to settle for less than what she truly deserves. Even when she's attracted to someone on her same professional level, the guy only seems to be interested in a Barbie doll look-alike or some other kind of exotic young chick that can't hold a decent conversation, but looks good on the arm. Zondra is biracial and beautiful to me, but I guess that because she's smart and well traveled and can hold her own on any topic, it's a turnoff to men who like to be the dominant force in a relationship instead of really appreciating what a partner like Zondra could bring to the table.

When Zondra does entertain men, her experiences always lead to the most comical escapades. I've gotten off of the phone with her so many nights dying of laughter about what she did to her man of the moment in the bedroom because she is a freak or her tale as to what kind of body malfunction the man had. Zondra is so funny, I thought it was a shame someone hadn't swept her off of her feet because she could definitely make some guy really happy.

CHAPTER 11

We arrived at Zondra's house, and immediately I was in awe at the way the place looked. She'd purchased a Colonial-style home from an auction that sat on two acres of land in a secluded upper-class area of Atlanta. Zondra took her time refurbishing the home, and it's one of the most attractive homes that I have ever seen. Zondra gave me a tour of the four bedroom, three bathroom home. Each room was designed with a different theme: her master bedroom was contemporary, while the guest rooms resembled China, an island in the Caribbean, and a village in Africa. I found each room to be more stunning than the last, which is how Zondra intended for anyone who was privileged to grace her home to react.

Once I'd recovered my breath from admiring her interior decorating, she escorted me to her outside garden that included several exotic flowers and a magnificent pond filled with tropical fish. Her gazebo was in a perfect place to curl up with a novel and enjoy the sounds of nature. Zondra's place was so mesmerizing that her home had been featured in *Better Homes & Gardens.*

Zondra explained that she had a well-known client who owned a landscaping company in addition to his recording studio, and he had offered to transform her property into a piece of heaven on earth as a token of appreciation for Zondra's representing him in a paternity case, which she'd handled discreetly without his current wife or the news media finding out. Zondra must have done a hell of a job on his behalf because I could never have dreamed of a better botanical oasis than the one in which I was currently standing.

Just as I was beginning to settle in, Zondra received an urgent telephone call and told me that she had to rush out. One of her clients had just been arrested, and she needed to head down to the local police station. I assured her I could manage on my own and I would just lose myself in her home until she returned.

After Zondra departed, I called Lance just to let him know I'd arrived in Atlanta safely. Once I finally reached him, he told me he was going to be busy while I was away; he had to select candidates to interview for a number of vacancies that had recently come open in the probation office. I told him about Zondra's lovely home, but my words couldn't express exactly what I saw, so I captured some pictures on my digital camera to let him see for himself. Before saying good night, Lance told me how much he loved me and that he wanted me to enjoy myself while I was away. I assured him that would be no problem in this sanctuary Zondra had created.

Just as I hung up with Lance, Zondra called to let me know she wouldn't be home until much later than she anticipated. If I wanted to go out and get something to eat, I could use her second vehicle which was in the garage; otherwise I could help myself to anything she had in the refrigerator or cupboards. I told Zondra I would just order something to be delivered but that I would wait up until she got back. I had a Terry McMillan novel I wanted to start reading, and this would be the perfect moment to begin.

It was close to midnight when Zondra finally got in, and she immediately began apologizing for ruining my first day with her. I told her I understood that her clients were important and that she must fulfill her duties as their attorney. Zondra looked exhausted. When she asked if I'd watched the local news, I told her no. She said, "I'll tell you why I was called away so suddenly. Don't think that I'm violating any attorney-client confidentiality because everything I tell you will be replayed on every local news station in Atlanta. I represent one of the most famous up-and-coming rap artists in Atlanta, and today he was arrested on possession of marijuana and drug paraphernalia charges."

"How did that happen?" I asked her.

"Apparently, he was initially stopped by the police for failure to come to a complete halt at a stop sign. He would just have gotten a warning if it weren't for the dizzy female he was riding with. She threw a Ziploc bag out of the window, which the officers say was filled with cocaine. Then she began to scream at the top of her lungs, "I don't want to go to jail—the drugs aren't mine!" The police officer radioed for additional assistance, then arrested everyone."

"So that's when he called you?"

"Yeah. I had to get to the precinct before the arrest hit the evening news."

Zondra was livid because the arrest would tarnish her client's reputation while the bad publicity could potentially ruin sales of his newly released album. At the police station, she was able to persuade the officers to take him immediately to court where she got him released on bond. I had to laugh at the picture Zondra was painting for me, I told her the "bad publicity" she was so concerned about just might catapult her client's career even further.

Zondra didn't find my statement amusing. "This means I'm going to have to work during your visit, and I'm not sure how much time I'll be able to spend with you, or if I'll really be able to show you my hometown."

I told her I wasn't worried about her entertaining me, shoot just being in a different atmosphere was more therapeutic for me than anything she might find for us to do. Besides, I had access to her BMW if I chose to sightsee. "You don't have to worry about me," I told her. "I can find numerous ways to amuse myself while you're busy."

CHAPTER 12

I got up real early on my third day in Atlanta, I wanted to get a jump-start on the day. I also wanted to have breakfast with my friend. But much to my surprise, Zondra was already up and out of the house before I made it to the kitchen. She'd left a note on the table: *Help yourself to anything, and if you need me, give me a call on my cell phone. Again, I'm sorry that I couldn't show you a good time today.* That girl worked entirely too hard, but she had to compete in a male-dominated profession, she had to go the extra mile just to prove she could run with the big boys. I just hoped she wouldn't burn herself out by working so much rather than taking time to smell the proverbial flowers.

It was easy finding my way around the city. I was able to identify several attractions that intrigued me. My most touching moment was when I went to visit the King Center. It was a remarkable opportunity to get a glimpse of what Dr. Martin Luther King, Jr. envisioned for African Americans. The King Center featured an educational tour of what life was like during the civil rights movement. MLK's dedication to equal rights for colored folks (that's what we were called during that time) and his stance on nonviolent protests were a testament to his courage and undying perseverance towards making a change in the world. All of the photographs displayed took me on an inspiring journey back in time. However, I was overcome with sadness as I thought about how life must have been for those who were a part of the struggle, and what Dr. King's views would be about the way African Americans behaved towards one another today.

The thought of Martin Luther King being disappointed in the state of the black community brought a river of tears to my eyes. He was a man who sacrificed the safety of his family, went to jail for his beliefs, marched on Washington DC, and ultimately gave his life so that a race of people could live the lives our Founding Fathers scripted in the U.S. Constitution: that every man should be afforded the right to life, liberty, and the pursuit of happiness. The King Center is a remarkable piece of history that is carefully preserved, one that changed me to the core of my being. I was overjoyed with the tremendous legacy it represented for the community and couldn't wait to tell Lance and Zondra all about my experience.

The next stop on my tour was the Centennial Olympic Park. Originally it had been built as a gathering spot for Olympic participants, area residents, and visitors to celebrate the 1996 Olympics. After the Olympics, the park was opened to the public, and now it's showcased as a restoration for business and community development in Atlanta.

I found this park to be twenty-one acres of the most beautiful landscaping I'd ever seen. Man, this was definitely peaceful. I enjoyed just walking and looking at the different people who had come to visit it. Too bad Zondra couldn't have joined me and enjoyed the scenery, but I captured the moment on my digital camera to share with her and Lance.

Today was my lucky day in visiting the park, they were having a Caribbean festival highlighting the various cultures of the islands. I sampled various foods, including Jamaican patties, jerk and curry chicken, rice and peas, mango salad, and champagne cola. Afterwards I was stuffed from all of the different foods; I couldn't help myself, everything was simply delicious. I then had to walk around the entire park just to burn off the calories I'd taken in.

Then I went from eating to buying souvenirs for my entire family, and I also picked up some things for Zondra. By the time I finished eating and shopping, I was exhausted so I returned to Zondra's home to rest until she came home from work. Atlanta had offered a variety of interesting leisurely pursuits, and I could see myself relocating to the state if the opportunity ever presented itself.

It was a long, hot day, and once I returned to the house, I took a bubble bath just to relax. Afterwards I fixed myself a sandwich and decided to kick back and watch television. I was flipping through the channels when the local news came on. I was so surprised from what I saw that I dropped my sandwich. Staring at me from the television was my best friend, Zondra. She was standing at a podium inside of the Dekalb County Police Station press room waiting to address the media regarding the pending charges against her client.

Now I knew Zondra had said the person she was representing was a popular rap artist, but I had no idea her client was MC Big Dane; even I was fond of a few of his hit singles. It turned out the woman who had been riding in the vehicle with him was the daughter of the Dekalb County police commissioner, and they were trying to charge MC Big Dane with possession of drugs. Obviously they were trying to somehow keep the daughter out of it.

It was amazing to watch Zondra in action. She said she'd obtained a copy of the video and audiotape from the dashboard of the arresting officer's vehicle, and she claimed they would prove her client's innocence as well as his cooperation throughout the entire process. She also indicated the tapes would show that the young lady involved was the one who was belligerent and that she had removed the bag containing the drugs from her blouse.

In response to Zondra's revelation, the attorney for the Sheriff's Office immediately came up to the podium and covered the microphone. He whispered something in Zondra's ear, and she announced, "In light of this new evidence, this press conference is cancelled so that the evidence can be reviewed and the authorities can determine how to proceed."

My girl was smooth, and she was obviously worth every penny she requested for her legal services. If it wasn't obvious to her law firm that she was firmly on the partnership track, then Zondra needed to think about starting her own law firm. I tried to call Lance and tell him Zondra was all of that, but my attempts to reach him were unsuccessful, and I ended up having to leave voice messages for him to return my calls. I started to worry a little because when he's not at work; Lance usually answers his cell phone.

Just as I finished my message on Lance's voicemail, Zondra walked through the door and exclaimed, "I'm yours, girl, for the remainder of your vacation!" Now it looked like her client would be cleared of all the charges, she could spend some time with me. Before I could suggest anything, Zondra told me we were going for a day at the spa which was her treat for my coming out to visit her and being so understanding regarding her work commitments. I reassured her that I truly understood that she had to pay the bills, so she better make that money, but I wasn't going to look a gift horse in the mouth, she'd get no arguments from me about paying for the spa.

CHAPTER 13

While I was enjoying my visit with Zondra, I was getting worried that other than a few quick conversations, I hadn't spoken to Lance since I'd arrived in Georgia. We really hadn't had any opportunity to talk, the few times I was able to catch him, he was moving at the speed of light. Either he was working really hard or he had to settle some problem his family was experiencing that they just couldn't solve without his input.

The one point of contention between Lance and me was his family. They were so exhausting; there was never a calm moment with them, and when a difficulty arose, it was always Lance to the rescue. Lance's mother, Ms. Cynthia, had a common-law husband, Mr. Milton; they had gotten together two years after Lance's father passed away after a long battle with diabetes. When their dad died, Lance was just fifteen years old and his little brother Richard was twelve. When Ms. Cynthia started shacking up with Mr. Milton, Lance couldn't wait to go away to college. He was infuriated that not only did his mother move her younger boyfriend into his dad's house, but Mr. Milton was a thug who wasn't interested in raising any children, especially since he had four kids of his own who he didn't claim.

Lance had told me all about his family when we got together, but when he described them, I thought he was exaggerating. I was willing to believe that Lance was upset with his mom because he didn't want anyone to take his father's place, but when he took me home, I quickly found out the picture he'd painted for me didn't even come close to what I witnessed. I'm not a psychotherapist, but after the few times I visited Lance's home, I've come to the conclusion that in the dictionary under the word *dysfunctional,* there must be a family portrait of the Weldon clan.

Now I've seen some crazy stuff in my short lifetime, but his family takes the cake. His mother pretended to be real cordial to me, but she always had a smart remark to make about me to Lance, and no matter how many times Lance told her what my name was, she kept calling me Shaunice, which was his ex-girlfriend's name. Now I know that *Denise* and *Shaunice* sound alike, but that woman knew good and well what my name was. If she was disrespectful towards me one more time, I planned to give her a piece of my mind.

I would have thought that his mother was just ill-mannered, but the rudeness didn't stop with her. Lance's little brother (and I use the term little only because of their ages) stood at 6'5" and weighed 265 pounds, Richard would come in and out of the house without even acknowledging his big brother even though he hadn't seen him in months. Now as big as he was, one would think he would be putting himself to some good use in athletics, but I guess that would be too constructive. The one reason he couldn't participate in sports like Lance did was because he was too busy making babies all over town. At nineteen, Richard had babies from two different girls with the children being born only four months apart—and that's just plain old *nasty*.

Then there was Mr. Milton (the young boyfriend); he never talked to me when I visited the house, but I would catch his ass staring at me from across the room while I was sitting on the couch and he was pretending to be watching television and drinking his six pack of beer. He could look all he wanted to—he was alright as long as he didn't put his hands on me.

If those weren't enough reasons for me to have anxiety about going to Ms. Cynthia's house, I could add that there was always some sort of catastrophe unfolding when we visited. I couldn't do anything except sit on the couch and observe. It would start with one of Richard's baby mamas dropping his kid off at the house but not advising anyone when she was going to return for the child. It wasn't unusual for me to end up babysitting during our entire visit. I made sure the children had a bath and were fed, then I entertained them to the best of my ability. I was happy to alleviate a little of the stress for Lance, even if it was just momentary. I think that's why Lance ultimately married me—he knew I was pretty good during a crisis. I was just holding it together for him, but truthfully, I dreaded going to visit his mom. It was extremely draining on all accounts: mentally, physically, and financially.

It was always something. Some of the things we had to contend with were: Richard having run up the telephone bill so the phone was about to be disconnected, Richard having just purchased a brand new vehicle that was going to be repossessed; the kitchen and bathroom sink being stopped up, his mom not having any money for groceries; they've missed payments at "Rent-A-Center" so the people were threatening to send them to collections and come pick up the furniture. Meanwhile I'm sitting back wondering, "What the hell is going on?" Here I am, I work every damn day and I can't afford a brand new car, yet this fool brother of his can walk on a car lot and drive away as a brand new owner. Then he has the nerve to pick up the telephone book looking for somebody to put some rims on his car and "pimp out" his ride by hooking up the stereo system and installing television sets in the headrests.

I don't know what kind of credit check these car salesmen were conducting, but surely somebody saw a sucker coming when they saw Richard and figured that at least they'd get their commission out of the deal.

I've also never known Richard to have steady employment, so as high priced as gasoline is nowadays, I didn't know who was putting the fuel in his tank for him to ride around town looking for a sperm bank recipient to make his latest deposit. Richard is so selfish he won't even drive his own kids around in his vehicle. Instead he uses his mother's car to transport them back and forth to the houses where their mamas live.

The funny thing is I'm the only one who seems to think something is wrong with this picture. Mr. Milton has his big ole rusty behind sitting up in that house letting Ms. Cynthia pay for everything; I would like to know what he was contributing to the household.

There was just no rationale behind some of the stunts they pulled, but Lance had to be the savior for all of them. I worried about it, but what could I do other than just sit back and watch the turmoil they caused my husband? When would it end? How could I truly express my thoughts and feelings to Lance without him becoming offended?

One source of comfort I did have when we went to Ms. Cynthia's house is that we didn't have to stay there overnight. I put an end to that the first time Lance took me home to meet his family during a spring break from college. When Lance said he wanted to introduce me to his family, I was excited; after all, when a guy takes you home to meet his mama, it means the relationship is going well.

Everything was fine until I had to go to the bathroom, which was the beginning of the end for me. I will never forget the day, once I finished my business in the bathroom, I flushed the toilet and it started to overflow, leaving me standing there trying to unclog the damn thing. There I was crying because I'd stopped up the toilet at Lance's mom's house, and Lance poked his head in the door to see why I'd been gone so long. He saw the expression on my face and the water all over the floor. He turned off the water and found a plunger to repair the damage, which is when we discovered that one of Richard's children had put a toy in the toilet. After that bathroom nightmare, I learned to hold my pee or bowel movements all day long until we got to the hotel where we were staying because I refused to go to the restroom in his mother's home. My excuse for not spending the night there was that I didn't feel right having sex in her house, so Lance never refused my request that we stay in a hotel during our visits since he knew that way he was going to get some loving.

With all of the warning signs Lance's family gave me, I still married his ass. I don't know who was crazier, them or me. Surely it must be me because

I'm the one who feels as if I need a couple of sessions on somebody's couch in order to get all of this off of my chest. I must have really been blinded by love, because this sure was a test of my marriage vows when it came to "for better or worse." Once you say "I do" to your spouse, you inherit those family problems, and there's no way you can escape being swept up into the dysfunction, especially when your husband has a big heart like Lance's. As his wife, I thought Lance should've set some boundaries as far as his family went so it wouldn't be such a big inconvenience every time some drama went down. However, he believed his duty was to fix all of the problems his mother and brother created, because if it wasn't for his dad's death, things wouldn't be this bad. I couldn't make him see things differently, so I just sat back and offered a supportive ear whenever he needed to vent his frustration.

When I finally got a chance to speak with Lance in depth during my trip to Atlanta, he said he was glad I had the opportunity to get away because he had to deal with so much over the past few days, and he knew that if he'd told me earlier about his family problems, I would have cancelled my trip and returned home to be by his side. He said that Richard had been arrested for possession of marijuana. His mother had been hysterical when she called him, cussing and fussing about how his dad would have been so disappointed in Richard, but she was glad that Lance turned out to be a good man. Ms. Cynthia had told Lance that she really needed help so that she could bail her "baby" out of jail. Lance had to send her the money via Western Union so Richard wouldn't have to spend the night in jail.

When Lance got a chance to speak with Richard, his brother told him that he'd been set up, and that the cops didn't have anything on him. Lance had to make a few phone calls to find out the truth because trying to decipher anything that his mother said or cross-examining his lying brother was a waste of time. Here my husband was, the chief federal probation officer, with a brother in the middle of a drug sting because he tried to purchase a dime bag of marijuana and some ecstasy pills from an undercover police officer. Lance had to call in some huge favors from some of his friends to get his brother's charges reduced to a misdemeanor, which meant that he would just have probation and pay a fine.

I was glad Lance hadn't called me about that foolishness. Yeah, I would've wanted to console and comfort him, but I would have let Richard's ass stay in jail for a few days just to scare him half to death. But there was Lance to the rescue once again. I could've ranted and raved about how his family only called when they wanted something, but it really wouldn't have mattered what I thought about the situation. Lance didn't have any limitations on what he would tolerate from his family, I believed their requests were a big intrusion on our lives and showed a total disregard for our relationship. They just didn't seem to care how their actions impacted our lives as well. However, Lance felt he was just doing everything his dad would have done if he were alive. Yeah, it was nice that Lance was a faithful son and brother, but when he saved them from every disaster, he was just enabling their actions which meant they wouldn't stop until they had us in the same boat with them—the one without a paddle. I was elated that I wasn't home to deal with them and I wasn't sure I would've been able to bite my tongue about Lance running to the rescue once again.

CHAPTER 14

I only had two more days to spend with Zondra before I had to return back to my busy life. She made good on her promise to treat me to a day at the spa. We went to the Jurlique Day Spa, located on Peachtree Road, where I felt I had died and gone to heaven. We both had a deep tissue Swedish massage and facials, then had our hair done at the beauty salon, and finished it off with a manicure and pedicure. Zondra and I laughed so hard during our pedicure, she told me how I'd fallen asleep during the massage session and started snoring so loud that she damn near fell off the table from laughing. Apparently I'd also started drooling on the floor when I turned on my front to have my back massaged. I told her she could laugh all she wanted, but hell, I felt like a million bucks—this day of pampering was long overdue.

Afterwards Zondra and I went back to her house to change for dinner, then she took me to Sean "P. Diddy" Combs' famous restaurant, Justin's, named after one of his many children. I'd been talking about the restaurant during my entire visit, and she said she'd been afraid I would never shut up about it, so she made reservations. We strolled right on by everyone else standing in that long-ass line wrapping around the building.

The experience was wonderful: the service was great, the portions were plentiful, and the atmosphere was relaxing. Everybody who thought they were somebody was up in there. Zondra got a lot of glances from attractive men, some who were even brave enough to come to our table and ask what we were drinking. Although we were asked to join two fine, sexy brothas at their table, Zondra politely declined. One of the guys responded by arching an eyebrow and giving us a suspicious look, apparently thinking that if we were turning them down, Zondra and I must be a couple of lipstick lesbians. I let it be known quickly that I don't flow like that by flashing my wedding ring. I was kind of relieved that I didn't have to go through the dating scene anymore, it was nothing more than a meat market where women still outnumbered the men ten to one. I asked Zondra how the hell did she date, and she said that she didn't as she was too busy establishing herself in the corporate arena.

There was one guy in the restaurant sitting at the bar, who kept looking at Zondra. My criminology background kicked in, and I said, "Girl, we're gonna have to slip out of this restaurant. I think you have a stalker undressing you with his eyes. He's over at the bar."

Being her silly self, Zondra turned around and made it obvious that I'd been talking about the man. She just laughed. "Girl, that's Stephen Marshall. He used to work at my firm, but he left about two years ago to start his own law practice. He's pretty good at what he does."

"It's just that he started to scare me," I told her. He was one of the ten white men in the room (I counted when we arrived) other than some of the wait staff. "But he is cute and kind of smooth looking."

"Yeah, he's smooth alright. He's has grown up with African Americans so he thinks he's an honorary member of the race."

I told Zondra that she was no spring chicken, and that she'd better stop playing hard to get and try "Something New" like Sanna Lathan did in that movie when she married a white guy. We just fell out laughing.

CHAPTER 15

My visit with Zondra had finally come to an end. She took me to the airport early in the morning, and we just stood there hugging each other like grapes on a vine. I really had missed seeing her and having her make me laugh at the silliest things, but I needed my husband something bad and I couldn't wait until my airplane landed in Fort Lauderdale. I wanted to show my man just how much he meant to me and help him relieve some of that pinned-up stress his mama and brother had caused while I was away. On my plane ride back home, I couldn't stop smiling to myself about my visit with Zondra, I made a vow that I was going to help her find someone special so that she didn't let her work become the most important thing in her life.

The flight was pleasant, and I was back in Florida before I knew it. I was excited about seeing my husband. The plan was for him to meet me in baggage claim and we would walk back to the car together. My luggage arrived quickly, so all I had to do was wait on Lance. I knew he was aware of what time my plane landed so I didn't start to worry until I'd been standing in the baggage claim area for almost an hour. When I called his cell phone, all I got was his voicemail. That concerned me, but I didn't want to turn into my mother, so I just requested a Super Shuttle to take me home.

On the way there, I kept trying to reach Lance, including calling our house phone, but he didn't answer there either. Now I was really worried, especially when I arrived home and saw his car was sitting in the driveway.

I entered the house and found Lance asleep on the couch in the entertainment room with the television on. I knocked his feet off of the couch and he jumped up, clearly startled. I told him, "I'm glad that you could catch up on your sleep since you forgot to come to the airport and pick your wife up who you haven't seen in a week."

Lance was very apologetic. He said he was exhausted and had lain down to take a nap and the time just slipped away. Since he looked so cute, I decided to accept his apology, and he rushed to hug and kiss me.

Instead of staying in that evening, Lance wanted to take me out to dinner to catch up on my visit with Zondra and to make up for leaving me stranded at the airport. We dined at one of my favorite restaurants, Hops in Pembroke

Pines. Over our dinner, he told me that interviewing new probation officers and dealing with his mom and brother had wiped him out. Richard was now doing better, and Lance thought he had been scared straight since his visit to jail and he'd figured out that was no place he wanted to spend his life. However, the experience had left his mother drowning her sorrows in alcohol. He said, "She spends the majority of the day drinking and the remainder of the evening looking through old photo albums, crying about how if my father hadn't died, things would be different, and Richard wouldn't get into so much trouble."

I could see the pain on Lance's face and the way these issues were taking their toll on him. I asked if his mother would be interested in seeking professional help for her drinking—someone with whom she could talk about the death of her husband.

Lance just laughed. "How can you help someone when they don't think there's anything wrong?"

We finished the rest of our dinner in silence. I didn't even dare mention the relaxing time I'd had with Zondra, it was obvious he needed some one-on-one time with his wife just to unwind and clear his head.

When we got back home, I didn't wait until we reached the bedroom—I pushed Lance up against the front door and kissed him hard on the mouth. I wanted to taste him and smell what I've been missing. He didn't resist when I took his shirt off and unbuttoned his pants. He stepped out of his shoes, and it was easy for me to remove my strapless dress. I sat Lance on the couch and gave him a striptease that had him panting like a dog. I put my head between his legs and teased him with my tongue; he arched his head back, put his hand on the back of my head, and said, "Baby, I've been missing you so much."

After I had Lance hard as a rock, I climbed on top of him. He buried his head between my breasts and found his way to my nipples, which was my weak spot. Lance scooped me up and put my back against the wall. He held onto my butt and started pumping his way to climax. He let out a scream so loud, I had to cover his mouth for fear the neighbors would think we were fighting.

After we were done, we collapsed on the floor and talked about how one week apart was far too long for us to go without seeing one another, but the reunion was worth the time apart. I went to sleep that night rubbing my husband's head in an attempt to soothe away his pain.

I would have really liked to give his mother and brother a piece of my mind, but I was afraid that it would only upset Lance further. He was so giving when it came to his family, but I don't think they really cared about how their actions stressed Lance out. I was almost convinced that his mom was just a master manipulator who called and cried just to play on Lance's sympathy. Well, she had one more time to deplete the energy out of my husband, then I was going to let her have it with both barrels. What they're doing to him made no sense, and it had to come to an end. Lance might get upset with me, but I wouldn't be a good wife if I didn't do everything in my power to protect him, even from his own mama and brother.

As I lay here next to my man while he was sound asleep, I made a solemn promise to myself that this would be the last crisis he was called upon to mend. From now on, his mother and brother were going to start pulling their own weight and getting their lives together. My plan sounds real good—now all I had to do was persuade Lance that he had to be the enforcer to put it into effect.

CHAPTER 16

It wasn't long before I got back into the swing of things at work. Things settled down in Lance's office as well once he made the selections for his new probation officers. I had no complaints as to how my life was turning out. Lance was interested in expanding our family soon, but I was more interested in establishing myself in my career and deciding what career path I wanted to take. Since the BOP promoted from within the agency, I had the opportunity to select from a number of departments, but I was unsure as to where I wanted to direct my attention the most.

What I did know was that I was uneasy that Lance kept pressuring me to have children; I couldn't digest the notion that I would have to be responsible for another human being. Plus, I wasn't ready to share Lance with anyone just yet. I know that sounds selfish, and it may be, but Lance's job kept him very busy. If we were to have children, I would be doing all of the work alone, and I didn't want to bring a child into the world under those circumstances. Despite my reservations about motherhood, Lance was always showing me baby clothes when we were out shopping or telling me about experiences our college friends were having with their children. Every now and again, Lance would catch me in a maternal moment, and I would daydream about what kind of person we could create with our genes and God's blessing, but I didn't think the moment was right.

When the holiday season was approaching, Lance felt the daddy bug the most. I think he secretly craved what he'd felt when his father was alive. Trust me when I say that between the ones his brother and my sister had, we had enough children in the family right now to keep us broke and exhausted from their visits to our house since they managed to break everything I considered precious. Therefore, having kids was not at the top of my "to do" list at the moment. I assured Lance that children would come in time, but he didn't want to hear any more excuses from me, and said he wanted us to talk seriously about expanding our family soon.

I had to think of something quick to get Lance's mind off of babies, so I persuaded him to go to the mall with me to look for a suit for his holiday party at work. Every year Lance tries to get me to accompany him to his work functions, but I always remind him of what happened with my gyrating co-worker at my Christmas party. The thought of that humiliating night is usually enough to get him to drop the subject. Besides, I don't want to be standing around with a fake ass smile on my face pretending to remember the names of people trying to impress their boss.

Despite my refusal to accompany Lance to this year's holiday party, I did enjoy helping him select a nice suit for the event. We went into Macy's to look in their men's department, and while Lance was trying on different combinations, I wandered off to the women's shoe section to pick out something for myself. I was busy trying on different shoes and didn't think about Lance until I heard his voice and the laughter of a female. I hurriedly returned to my husband and found him engaged in conversation with a person I knew from college.

When he saw me, Lance said, "Hey, honey—I know you remember Rebecca Bennett."

I smiled. "How could I forget her?" Then I gave Rebecca the once-over glance, and she gave me a fake hug, exclaiming that it had been far too long since we'd seen each other.

As we chatted, she indicated that she was in the store shopping for a dress to wear at her office party. "Where do you work now?" I asked her.

Rebecca looked back and forth from me to Lance. He swallowed hard and said, "Honey, I forgot to mention that one of the people I interviewed for a position in my office was Rebecca. Now she works for me."

"Oh," I said. Lance excused himself and went into the fitting room leaving me standing there with Rebecca—someone whom I've never been particularly fond of. Rebecca said that she was in a hurry, but she looked forward to seeing me again and catching up on old times. Yeah, I bet she did.

When Lance came out of the fitting room, he smiled and asked, "Are you OK?"

"Sure—why wouldn't I be? And by the way, we're not done shopping, since I've decided to attend this year's Christmas party with you after all."

Lance just smiled and said, "Sure, let's get something for my baby to show just how hot you are." Little did he know I wasn't interested in attending the party for his benefit—I just wanted to keep an eye on that slut Rebecca. She was slick as grease, and I knew firsthand that she was one of those females who would do just about anything to get ahead.

CHAPTER 17

Rebecca Bennett had attended the University of Florida with Lance and me. She was my teammate on the track team. Rebecca lived in Miami, and even though she was a year behind me, I used to run into her during local track meets when we were in high school. I remember that she was really good in high school, but she got pregnant and didn't run her senior year. However, she still received a full scholarship because she was talented and our coach decided to give her another chance. She competed as a heptathlete, meaning she didn't stand out in one event, but she was good in seven events combined.

There was always something about her that made me suspicious of her. Although I was always friendly towards her, I kept her at a distance. I was her host when she came to visit the university as a recruit. I found out then that we didn't have anything in common except for track and field and being from Miami.

Even though being around Rebecca made me uneasy, I showed her what life was like on campus and introduced her to numerous people. I tried to expose her to a little of everything the college had to offer. I must have done a hell of a job, because by the end of her visit, Rebecca had made up her mind to accept a scholarship at U of F. I told her that selecting a college was a big decision and suggested she should visit some other schools that were closer to home, because she might miss her child if she chose to live in Gainesville.

Then I came right out and asked her who was going to raise her child. You would have thought I'd insulted her. She said, "For your information, my mom will be taking care of my daughter while I'm away at college." Apparently, she was the first one in her family to attend college, and her mother didn't want the fact that Rebecca had a child to limit her possibilities. I understood all of that, but one thing that struck me as odd was Rebecca's comment, "Besides, getting away from Miami will give me a chance to be free once again." That made me doubt I could have a friendship with her. I mean, what kind of mother wants to dump her child off on her own mother and try her best to forget all about the baby?

As it turns out, being an unfit mother wasn't her only character flaw. She turned out to be a backstabbing, low-down tramp. As much as I hated to listen to my mother, one thing she said always sticks out in my mind: "Trust your instincts." Instinctively I knew there was something about Rebecca that I didn't like or trust.

My high school sweetheart was Carl Lemon; he also accepted a scholarship at the University of Florida as a star fullback on the football team. He and I had been inseparable throughout high school, and I thought he was "the one" until he did something to me that I could never forgive him for.

One evening, track practice was cancelled because it was raining; the coach didn't want anyone to get sick, so she allowed us to take the remainder of the day off to study and rest. I thought I could spend the night with Carl since he lived off campus in an apartment that he shared with a teammate. Before I went to Carl's, I stopped by the grocery store to pick up a few things I wanted to cook for dinner, especially since I knew he never had any good food in the refrigerator. When I got to Carl's apartment complex, the security guard just waved me through the gate since it was raining so hard and he was used to seeing me in the complex; he didn't telephone Carl to let him know I was arriving.

Making my way upstairs with an armful of groceries in the pouring rain proved to be difficult, but I had the key to Carl's place so I let myself in. I planned to start dinner immediately so that later I could relax and snuggle with Carl.

When I got into the apartment, I noticed that Gerald LaVert's CD was playing on his stereo. I thought *OK, I need to be quiet because it looks as if Carl's roommate Chris had some company and is getting his groove on.* I quietly placed my car keys and groceries on the counter and decided to go to Carl's room and watch television.

As I approached his bedroom door, I heard soft moans coming from inside. It was then that I felt my stomach get queasy. I opened his bedroom door and saw Rebecca Bennett on her knees in my boyfriend's bed with him behind her having sex doggie-style.

All I remember doing is standing there waiting for Ashton Kutcher to come out of the closet to let me know that I was being "Punk'd" and that this was really all a big joke. When that didn't happen, I started crying and screaming at Carl, "How could you do this to us?" Carl turned around and saw me; he jumped out of bed and grabbed a pair of shorts and tried to come after me. I ran out of the room but not before I saw a grin on Rebecca's face.

I don't know how I made it back to campus, because between the rain and my tears, the road was a complete blur. Carl tried relentlessly to contact me all night long, but I avoided him. The next morning he was waiting outside my dorm building, but I didn't want anything to do with him anymore. I didn't have any respect for him and I couldn't even look at him. This fool had the nerve to follow me to my class and ask me, "Niecey, is this the end of us?"

I almost fell out laughing. I turned around and asked him, "If you saw some other dude driving his dick in me, would you want to still be with me?" He stood there with his mouth open. I said, "Exactly. And don't call me any more." Those were the last words I spoke to Carl, and after that I did my best to avoid him.

As for Rebecca, it was hard trying to avoid her, she was my teammate and I had to see her at practice daily. I really didn't want to be around her after I overheard her in our locker room after practice a few days after the incident. She was talking to another teammate, laughing about me catching her with my boyfriend. She said I obviously wasn't giving Carl what he needed because she'd had him moaning and screaming her name.

I made my presence known to Rebecca and advised her that she could have Carl. "Remember the same way that you got him will be the same way that you lose him. Besides, the only reason that Carl is with you is because I wouldn't take his ass back, and if you like my seconds, you're welcome to him."

She looked so smug as she said, "I doubt that Carl will be going anywhere. If you knew how to satisfy your man, it wouldn't have been so easy for me to get him."

I got so mad, I jumped up in her face and said, "A bitch like you will get just what you deserve!"

Zondra was there, and she grabbed me and said, "Please don't do anything that would get you expelled, girl—neither Carl nor Rebecca are worth it." Zondra was right, but I was so mad, I just wanted someone to hurt as bad as I was hurting.

Five months later, someone *was* hurting as bad as I was, but I would never wish harm on anyone. It just so happens that Carl and Rebecca actually started dating after I caught them in bed together. But I could tell that Carl was miserable, he still called me all the time or passed messages through Zondra to relay to me. I was getting on with my life and I wished that he would do the same. Knowing that Carl was with Rebecca made me want to vomit every day, but if that's where he wanted to be, then so be it. Rebecca wasn't a female who had his best interests at heart, and she wouldn't be able to pretend forever. Her true colors would eventually shine and Carl would regret the day he ever met her.

The day I heard the awful news about Carl, I couldn't help but think it was more like karma coming back to dish out the same pain which he caused me—that is until I heard the entire story. During football practice, Carl was going through his running drills when he was tackled by a swarm of defensive players. Once everyone got up off of him, he tried to get up too, but his ankle was twisted the wrong way and he fell back down on the ground. When Carl looked at his ankle, he went into shock and they had to rush him to the hospital for emergency surgery.

Now I was still upset at him, but I was not mean spirited; I empathized with him knowing how much pain he would be in. I also knew his recovery phase would be long and hard; having to undergo surgery for my knee made me a little more understanding about the long road to healing that Carl was about to embark upon. I went to the hospital as soon as I heard about him only to run into Rebecca who was in the recovery room standing by Carl's bed. I was cool with his best friend and his coach even knew me so they let me stay in the room. When the doctor came in, we all stood up and waited for him to tell us Carl's prognosis, but the expression on the physician's face told me it wasn't going to be good.

As it turns out, Carl had broken his ankle so badly that he'd torn all of the ligaments and tendons in it. The doctor said that he had done all that he could do to save the foot, but Carl would never be able to play football again.

Carl started crying, and Rebecca said, "What? There's no way I'm staying with you now, especially since you aren't going to the NFL." She gathered up her belongings and rushed out of the hospital, leaving us standing there astonished at her lack of compassion. I could have yanked the weave out of that silly girl's head, but I don't think that it would have done much good. I just smiled at Carl and told him that he was going to be just fine, and it was up to him to prove the doctors wrong about his future.

Carl surprised everyone when he defied the future his doctor predicted. He persevered by sweating through a grueling eight months of rehabilitation, eventually making it back onto the football field where he broke every school record for his position. Not only did he lead the Gators to a national championship, but after we graduated he was a second round draft pick of the New Orleans Saints. Rebecca had ruined her chance with him by revealing that she was nothing more than a gold-digging ho. She didn't know the Carl I knew: someone who would do whatever it took to play football again.

CHAPTER 18

Even though Lance knew all about my history with Rebecca, he still hired her. I was pretty angry with him. He was adamant with me, saying the only reason he'd chosen her was because she was one of the few qualified candidates who'd applied. I knew that I was just upset about what had happened between Rebecca and me in the past, but he assured me it had honestly slipped his mind. I couldn't stay mad at Lance no matter how hard I tried, so I decided to just forget all about Rebecca, but you can best believe I was going to be on point when I showed up at Lance's office holiday party.

By the time the Christmas party rolled around, I was actually excited about attending with Lance. I had an appointment with Deborah so that she could hook my hair up for the party. When I needed to look nice, Deb never disappointed me. I showed up at Deb's salon with various photos of the different hairstyles I was thinking about. Deb looked at the sample photos and said, "Look, I know that I do a good job, but I'm not a magician. You might as well put those pictures away because I already know how I'm going to style your hair. It's going to look so good that you and my brother-in-law just might not make it to the party."

I just laughed at my big sister and told her, "When you're done with me, I better look like a million bucks." Just for me being smart with her, Deb turned my chair away from the mirror so I couldn't see how she was styling my hair until she finished. When I finally was able to look in the mirror, Deb had pinned my hair up in a way that had twists and spirals cascading down the sides of my head. She'd added her own special touch by putting this shimmering sheen on that made me simply dazzling. That girl knew that she could do some hair. Deb said that my hairdo was on the house—her gift to me since we didn't see each other that much. I couldn't wait to get home and show it off to Lance.

When I arrived, Lance was just pulling up in the driveway. He got out the car and asked, "Is this the foxy lady I will have the pleasure of escorting this evening?"

I said, "Indeed it is, sir, so you'd better treat her right."

"Always." Lance liked my hair so much he thought he could persuade me to have sex without messing it up. But I told him I didn't think so because I'd sat under the hair dryer entirely too long for him to be messing it up. He was just going to have to understand that I was not about to sweat out my hair.

Getting ready for Lance's holiday party was so much fun. When we dressed up and stepped out together, we really complemented one another. Lance loved the dress that I'd picked out. It was a backless, form-fitting red one that stopped at my knees and looked so good against my light brown complexion. With my hair pinned up, I could have been a movie star getting ready for an awards ceremony. Lance looked very handsome in his suit from the Steve Harvey Collection that had been tailored to fit him perfectly; it was black with a white shirt and a red tie to match my dress. When we finally got dressed, we were ready to go dancing. I hadn't eaten anything all day, I was hungry as hell and I couldn't wait until we got to the party.

When we arrived at the hotel ballroom, it was better than I had expected. I was glad I'd decided to accompany Lance, and his employees weren't annoying at all. Lance and I danced, but I couldn't get my boogie on like I wanted to. I wanted to "drop it like it was hot" or "scrub the ground," but it wasn't that kind of party. This was a classy affair, and I wasn't going to be dancing like one of Luther "Skywalker" Campbell's video girls.

Lance really decided to enjoy the night—so much so that he drank a little too much by my standards. I tried to remind him that he was in the company of his subordinates, and it wasn't a good idea for them to see him sloshed. Lance agreed with me and had stayed sober long enough to let me know that he had gotten us a room at the hotel so we didn't have to drive all the way back home. He gave me one of the keys to the room just in case I wanted to leave the party before him.

It was getting late and some people had started going, but I was having such a good time, I didn't want the night to end. I was enjoying the party so much that I didn't even notice when Rebecca walked into the room with a dress on that looked like it was big enough for a five-year-old. I don't know where that hussy thought she was going dressed like that. She looked as if her pimp had just dropped her off so that she could stroll for johns to pick her up. I tell you, there are hood rats everywhere.

It was 2:00 a.m. before I realized the party was shutting down. I was talking and having such a good time, I didn't even notice that Lance had disappeared. I figured he must have gone upstairs to the hotel room to sleep off some of the alcohol. I hoped he'd gotten some rest, because now I was ready for him mess up my hair.

I grabbed my purse and headed to the elevators. As I got off the elevator, I found the key to Room 1482, which was at the end of the hall; I silently put my card in the door slot and opened the door. I had an uneasy feeling as I heard whispers in the dark. I could hear my husband's voice saying, "Baby, you feel so good. Why do you do this to me, Denise?"

If he's supposed to be talking to me, and I'm standing in the doorway, then who the hell is making him feel so good? As I rounded the corner, I had a sense of déjà vu. When I turned on the light, for the second time in my life, I saw was Rebecca Bennett's ass. She was straddled across my husband in a way that I was used to covering him. My heart jumped into my throat and I screamed, "What the hell is going on?"

At the sound of my voice, Lance's eyes got as big as saucers. "Niecey, I thought that she was you."

"Well, you thought wrong!" I grabbed the car keys off the nightstand. "Don't bother coming home because you don't have a home with me any more."

Rebecca had gotten up and gone over to the sink to get a glass of water. I said, "I knew you were a dirty bitch, but why do you want to be me so bad?" I must have struck a chord with her because she aimed the glass at my head and threw it.

Lance jumped off of the bed and stood between the both of us with his dick just hanging and swinging. I could've slapped the shit out of him for being so stupid. He said, "Can we talk about his like adults?"

"Hell to the no, you can have this bitch. I'm out of here." I swung the door open so fast, I almost dislocated my arm. Lance was trying to yell after me not to leave because he couldn't get dressed quick enough to follow me. Meanwhile I could hear Rebecca telling him that she could make him happier than I ever could.

Lance told her to get away from him, and she replied, "Be careful what you ask for, boss—I could make things real uncomfortable for you at work. Especially since the federal government has a zero tolerance for sexual harassment in the workplace." All I could think about as I left the hotel with Lance standing in the hallway was he sure sobered up when he got caught in the act.

CHAPTER 19

I couldn't stay in the same house with Lance that night. He had to make alternate plans, especially since I'd taken the car; he had no way of getting home. For all I cared, he and that lousy tramp Rebecca could finish what they had started. I knew that I would never forgive him for having sex with that slut.

Once I left the hotel, I called Deborah, but she couldn't understand anything I was saying because I was crying so hard. She called Diane, and we all spoke on a three-way call. I vividly replayed the scene I'd witnessed between Lance and Rebecca. They were both ready to come over and whip his ass, then ambush Rebecca with a towel soaked in gasoline so we could take her somewhere to beat the crap out of her and leave her for dead. I knew that they were just trying to protect me, but the truth is both of them were soft as marshmallows. If we were caught doing something, it wouldn't take the detectives long to get a confession out of either of them. As much as I appreciated them for trying to defend my honor; I just needed their help with packing up some of my belongings from my house.

The next morning Lance got to the house just as Deb and Diane pulled up with a U-Haul van. He ran into the house and said, "Denise, don't leave me—we can work things out. I was drunk, and I thought she was you." That statement just made me pack faster. I told him he could forget about being my husband because I could never look at him without seeing her on top of him. I couldn't believe that he'd had sex with the one person I despised more than anyone in this world. I also advised him I would be starting divorce proceedings first thing in the morning, and it would be in his best interest not to contest it, since most judges frowned upon infidelity.

It's amazing what you can accomplish through anger and rage. With my sisters helping me, I cleaned out my house in three hours. Until I decided what I was going to do, I made plans to move in with my parents, telling them it would be until the divorce was final and I was free of my cheating husband. Now I had to prepare myself to break the news to them, and I wasn't looking forward to their interrogating me about the events of last night. My mind was reeling with thoughts of Lance and Rebecca together. Not only did he ruin our marriage, but he could possibly have ruined his career as well, all over a piece of ass.

I'm not much of a drinker, but I didn't think there was any way in the world that he could have mistaken her for me. I'm his wife—how could he not tell the difference? I'd been sharing a bed with this man for years, yet he allowed another woman to violate what was supposed to be something sacred between us. It made me so ill just to think about their tryst, and the sight of him made me want to punch him in the face. I felt like a complete fool. Rebecca had done this to me once before. How could it be happening again? My entire life had been destroyed in a matter of minutes, with everything I thought was safe and special now having become obsolete.

I had to figure out what to do next. This city wasn't big enough for me to avoid the both of them. I was afraid if I came in contact with either of them, I might do bodily harm to someone and land myself in jail.

CHAPTER 20

My parents were waiting for me when I arrived with my sisters. As it turned out, I didn't have to explain anything: Deborah with her big-ass mouth had already told them what happened, and of course because she's so melodramatic, she'd embellished the story so my parents had her version instead of the true one. I didn't even have the energy to get into details with them; I was so exhausted, and I knew I couldn't explain everything again without crying like a newborn baby.

When the dust finally settled, my mom came into my old bedroom and tried to talk to me. She said, "You know, Denise, we all make mistakes, and maybe you are rushing to judgment without giving Lance an opportunity to explain what really happened."

I looked at her like she had just bumped her head. "Mom, how could I look at him the same way without being reminded of what I saw? I just can't feel the same way about him, knowing that he was with another woman."

All she could say was, "Denise, everything isn't always as it appears to be."

"I'm not in the mood for trying to figure out any of your riddles right now. All I know is that I saw my husband having sex with another woman, and I'm not going back to him."

For the next eight months, my mother kept trying to persuade me to give Lance another chance. She went as far as quoting Bible scriptures to me. But she was in for a fight because I gave it right back to her. She came to my room one evening and said, "Denise, I raised you to fight, and I don't want a daughter of mine running when she's faced with a battle."

I told her that she could fight all she wanted to, but I wasn't willing to fight for anyone who was so easily coaxed into committing adultery. I didn't care how much she talked to Lance and listened to his side of the story. JoAnn wasn't listening to anything that I had to say about leaving Lance; whatever the problem, she was all for sticking it out.

Once I let her know she was wasting her time and breath trying to talk me into staying with Lance, the gloves came off. She went from motherly advice to quoting scriptures to me. It started with Malachi 2:16: "'For I hate divorce,' says the Lord, the God of Israel."

"Umm, he also said in Exodus 20:14, 'Do not commit adultery.'

Then she hit me with I Corinthians 13:5–7:

Love does not demand its own way. Love is not irritable, and it keeps no record of when it has been wronged. It is never glad about injustice but rejoices whenever the truth wins out. Love never gives up, never loses faith, is always hopeful, and endures through every circumstance.

I gave it right back to her when I told her Hebrews 13:4 says, "Give honor to marriage, and remain faithful to one another in marriage. God will surely judge people who are immoral and those who commit adultery."

But Mom wouldn't quit. She said to me to look at I Corinthians 7:10: "Now, for those who are married I have a command that comes not from me, but from the Lord. A wife must not leave her husband."

"Oh yeah. What about a little earlier at first Corinthians chapter 6, verses nine through ten? That says

Don't you know that those who do wrong will have no share in the Kingdom of God? Don't fool yourselves. Those who indulge in sexual sin, who are idol worshippers, adulterers … none of these will have a share in the Kingdom of God.

This went on for about an hour, until my mom was so pissed off that she stormed out of my room and told me to quit twisting God's words. I chuckled to myself and said a silent prayer of thank you for her making me attend Sunday school and learning the Bible.

Living with my parents while my divorce was finalized made me want to get as far away from them as I possibly could. Pops was alright, as he tried to be supportive in his own way; his hugs did the trick when I was feeling really sad about what was going on between Lance and me. On the other hand, my mom just would not stop with her ranting and raving, and I'd had just about enough of her.

Plus Lance kept calling and coming over to the house to try and talk to me and let me know that he wanted a chance to gain my trust back. But giving him a chance wasn't even an option for me. My mom could plead his case, and Lance could beg and cry as much as he wanted, but I wasn't interested in mending any broken fences with him. Instead I wanted to get as far away from him and Miami as I could. I hadn't done anything wrong, but they were acting as if I were the one who had lost my mind.

If there had been a chance for Lance and me to reconcile, it was ruined the day I received an envelope in the mail that contained a sonogram photo with the words, "Thought you should know," written on the bottom. It was from Rebecca informing me that she was expecting a baby. That revelation put the nail in the coffin for me, and I put in for a job transfer. As soon as the opportunity presented itself, I was taking the first thing smoking out of Miami. If I'd stayed around here, I would end up jeopardizing my job because Rebecca would've made me hurt her, and besides what good would it do? For some reason she despised me and took pride in going out of her way to humiliate me.

I wouldn't allow Rebecca to get the best of me. She might have stolen two men away from me, both of whom I thought were something special, but in a way I felt sorry for women like her. They were envious of other women and they found some sense of sick satisfaction in breaking up a happy home. Women like Rebecca obviously didn't have a man in their lives like my daddy. I don't deal with people like her, and when I think of all the pain that she has caused me, another one of my mama's famous Bible quotes from Galations 6:7 echoes in my ears: "You will reap what you sow."

CHAPTER 21

Lance didn't contest the divorce, and it was finalized within a year. The attorney I hired assured me that since we didn't have any kids and the only joint property that we shared was the house we'd purchased together, it would be simple. The house was being sold, and once the papers were signed, I would be free. I'd compare getting a divorce to experiencing the death of a family member—your heart aches for the person you lost, but life goes on. As painful as it was, this was a relationship I had to bury because there was no way it was coming back to life.

There were so many mixed emotions flowing through my body as I stood in the courtroom listening to the judge order the dissolution of my marriage. I was numb, and I said a silent prayer to God: *let this be the start of something good for me because I have been through so much in the past year, and I think I'm at my breaking point.*

God must have been smiling on me because once I left the courthouse from my divorce proceedings; I got a telephone call from my shift supervisor at the prison. He told me he had some good news for me and he didn't want to prolong the news; he told me that I had been selected as a correctional counselor at FCI-Williamsburg, South Carolina. I couldn't believe my ears, and I told him that yes, I wanted the position. I knew then that God was answering my prayers as this was definitely a sign that things for me were about to change for the better. As for my ex-husband, he looked so broken when I left him standing in front of the courthouse, but I was broken the night I'd caught him with another woman, the same one who was taunting me with their having created a life together.

Lance had done his best to try and persuade me that the child Rebecca was carrying was not his, but I didn't even care. The mere fact that he'd put himself in such a compromising position was enough for me to be disgusted at the sight of him. However, I knew that this entire ordeal has taken its toll on him. He looked as if he had lost at least twenty pounds and hadn't been sleeping at all. I've never seen Lance like this before. I still cared about his well-being, but not enough to take his silly ass back. I was moving on with my life, the federal government was paying for my relocation expenses, and I was elated at the fact that my life was moving in a new direction.

Perhaps moving to South Carolina and experiencing a little bit of southern hospitality would allow me to forget all of the hurt I was feeling from Lance's act of betrayal, and maybe then I could learn to forgive without hardening my heart against those that have wronged me. My family was sad to see me go, but they understood I needed a change of atmosphere in order to start over again.

As I got ready to go, Pops said, "Remember you're a Martin—you don't owe anyone any excuses for the decisions you make in your own life. You only have one life to live, and you have to be happy, so make your own destiny, baby girl, and make me proud." I wanted to start crying, but I had no more tears to shed. Pops was right: it was time for me to put myself first and do the things I wanted to do.

The entire family had dinner together before I got on the road and headed for South Carolina. My sisters promised to visit for the holidays and to try to persuade my parents to make the eight-hour drive with them. I wasn't holding my breath on that one, but who knows? They might get brave and come see me.

CHAPTER 22

When I moved to South Carolina, I experienced an extreme culture shock. Talk about going backwards, this looked like the town of Mayberry. I ended up in the city of Salters, in Williamsburg County. Nothing reminded me of Miami: there were only two movie theatres and one mall, and the happening spot turned out to be the Wal-Mart Superstore. I spent so much time there trying to decorate my new townhouse that I should have bought stock in the company. While there really wasn't anything exciting about Salters, it was home for now, and I had to make the best of it. Settling into my new place gave me something to do and helped divert my thoughts off of everyone and everything I'd left behind.

Now Salters was out in the country, and the new prison where I would be employed was built in a swamp. I don't know who had done the scouting for land when the government purchased this property, but he needed his ass whipped. There was wildlife all over the place. I guess what they say is true: "Be careful what you wish for."

It appeared as though the federal government had been buying up land all over the nation in desolate areas and building correctional facilities to house federal inmates who had previously been housed in local or state facilities. When I initially accepted my position with the BOP, I'd been told that the best way for me to get promoted was to relocate, so maybe this move was the beginning of a promising future. The new prisons being built gave BOP employees an opportunity to move up the career ladder swiftly, and if any of my co-workers were like me, having these new prisons also gave them a chance to escape their pasts.

It was easy settling into my new position as a correctional counselor. I was assigned to the federal prison camp that only had 125 inmates. It was better than being inside the fence where the inmates were a little more rowdy. At the camp, they were at the end of their sentences, and not too many were interested in getting any infractions that would prolong their stay.

The inmates in my unit generally had between five months to five years to serve, and they had been around long enough to know not to come and bother me with trivial requests. I know that I was mean when I first arrived, but I had just come from a different kind of atmosphere in Miami where we had a mixture of every kind of criminal element. Besides, I just didn't trust convicts—I know just how manipulative they can be, and I had enough training to know the ways they try to persuade staff members to bring in contraband such as food, cigarettes, alcohol, or drugs. In general I've learned to keep inmates at a distance, as to not get caught up in a scandal that could jeopardize my job or land me in prison just like them.

My workdays were routine, but between my new position and decorating my new home, I had plenty to keep me busy. I had been in South Carolina for almost a year before I really started to feel lonely. I'd met a lot of new co-workers, but I was real hesitant to befriend anyone, primarily because I didn't want anyone all in my business. I was now single, and because I didn't fraternize with anyone at work, the rumor quickly got started that I was a lesbian. I don't know who was worse to be around, the inmates or the staff members. If that's what they thought, then that suited me—I was all about getting my paycheck and trying to figure out where to go from there.

The slow pace of living in the country as opposed to the big city allowed me to get involved with my community. I became a tutor for the local literacy group, and I joined the church and started singing in the choir. Slowly, I began to feel as if a change was taking place within me. Once I rededicated myself to God, I had a change of heart about the way I'd handled things with my ex-husband. I was no longer angry with him, and I had forgiven him for his actions. Now just because I had a forgiving heart didn't mean that I was willing to take him back, which definitely was not going to happen.

For the first time in a long while, I was on my own, and I liked being independent and discovering things about myself, but I would be telling a stone-cold lie if I said I didn't miss having a man to hold me and keep me warm on cold nights. I liked the idea of being married, but I'd been with one man for so long that I had no clue as to where to start searching for an eligible bachelor who came with the long list of attributes for which I was now looking.

I didn't hang out in nightclubs—I knew they were a meat market, and the men there weren't my idea of eligible bachelors. When I shared my desires with Zondra, she said not to ask her for advice, because if she had the answers, she would also have the man of her dreams. She's the one who persuaded me to service myself when I was feeling horny. I couldn't do anything but laugh at that girl, she said, "You're laughing, but it does the job, and you don't have to worry about STDs or anybody cheating on you." No matter how bad I was feeling, that girl could always say something to make me laugh. While she was playing, I was being serious about stepping out on the dating scene again. I wasn't in any hurry to snag a man, but I did want to start going out.

After I hung up the telephone after talking with Zondra, the first thing I did was to write down on a sheet of paper everything I wanted in a man. I stuck it in my Bible, trusting that God would give me exactly what I asked for. However, while I was waiting on the Lord to grant my request, I had to live in the moment and get out of fantasy land. For right now, I had to be content with how my life was going. Despite all that I'd been through, I was still standing, and I thought that said a lot about my character. In the midst of trouble, I'd made it through just fine, and I was mentally stronger than I ever thought I could be.

CHAPTER 23

I liked my new job, but I didn't think I would be doing so much work. I used to think that being a counselor was the best-kept secret as far as positions went in the BOP as my position would give me the flexibility to hide from inmates when I didn't want to be bothered, but I was actually doing more work than I was accustomed to. My duties included completing inmate visiting lists and telephone lists, picking up supplies for the housing unit, assigning jobs to the inmates, developing motivational classes—it just didn't stop.

Just when I thought I already had too much work to do, all the employees were called to an emergency meeting in which the Warden advised us that due to the threat of Hurricane Katrina striking the Gulf Coast, we had to prepare to receive a mass exodus of inmates who were being evacuated from Beaumont, Texas and sent to South Carolina. No one was ready for this news, and the prison was not equipped to receive inmates just yet. We were still activating the facility, with medical services, food service, laundry, and commissary department not being fully staffed; how could we accommodate the additional six hundred inmates who were due to arrive by the end of the week? Regardless of whether we were ready, we were told to prepare for their arrival with everyone working overtime until all of the inmates were properly screened and assigned to their housing units.

All I could think was *damn, Hurricane Katrina had an affect not just on the residents of Louisiana, Texas, and Mississippi, but all over the nation.* The BOP had to make sure the inmates were safe from all harm during this natural disaster. I just knew I was in for a long weekend. I'd just gotten my period, I was already in a foul mood, and this announcement of our impending new commits did little to change it, I knew these inmates would be bringing with them a bunch of other problems the institution wasn't equipped to solve.

I've been in this line of profession long enough to know that inmates are creatures of habit, and once you take them out of their natural surroundings; it's just a matter of time before disaster occurs. My experience and intuition told me that we were going to be dealing with a different kind of criminal element with these Texas inmates. The majority of the inmates who were coming to South Carolina were affiliated with a gang, such as the Mexican Mafia, the Suenos, Texas Syndicate, Dirty White Boys, Aryan Brotherhood, Bloods, Crips, and Black Gangsta Disciples. I didn't expect a bunch of Boy Scouts, but I also knew the staff at FCI-Beaumont would take this opportunity to empty out their trash and disburse it all over the southeastern region in an attempt to clean house by getting rid of their "problem children."

Before the inmates arrived at FCI-Williamsburg, they made a pit stop at another in-transit facility, USP Atlanta. That was another part of the filtering process. During that stop, inmates were transferred or redesignated to other facilities, so by the time the buses arrived in South Carolina, it was mass confusion to say the least.

As a correctional counselor, one of my job duties was to screen new inmates to determine if they were able to join the general inmate population. If it was determined they would be a nuisance within the general population, or they had issues such as being an active gang leader or charged with sexual abuse, then we had to house them in segregation until their status was reviewed by a correctional supervisor.

When the first inmate stepped off of the bus, I knew I was in for a long weekend. We couldn't even get the inmates fingerprinted before the questions started. It began with complaints about when they were going to eat, when they would get their personal property, when they could buy items off of the commissary list, and when they would be able to talk to their families and advise them of their whereabouts. I was so mentally and physically exhausted that my patience was as long as frog's hair—that is, real short.

Before I blew a fuse on an inmate, I reminded myself that I received a good paycheck and I could be doing something worse; therefore I should be grateful for the job. But once you've answered the same question two hundred times in one night, you're just about ready to scratch somebody's eyeballs out, and you don't care who they belong to. Plus with these inmates traveling all day long, some hadn't had a shower, and many must have forgotten to run past a toothbrush before they got on the bus, because I swear that when I spoke to most of them, their breath almost singed off the hair on my eyebrows.

By the time Sunday rolled around and we were almost done with the last bus, I didn't think I could listen to anyone else; I was busy trying to figure out how fast I could get home and take a nice long bubble bath. When I took a break, my supervisor looked at me and asked how I was feeling; the only thing I could think of was *here's my opportunity to leave.* I told my supervisor that I was having really bad cramps, and I didn't think that I could stay any longer (that line never seems to fail).

My supervisor said, "Just screen the last inmate for the camp and then you can take off."

I said, "Alright, boss." With my plan for escape approved, all I had was one more inmate who had been assigned to the camp to be socially screened. It had been a long weekend for everyone, inmates included, and I was glad I was going to get to run when I had the chance.

Prior to speaking with any of the new commits, I always reviewed their pre-sentence investigation reports to find out why they had been convicted, and I learned about their personal lives since they weren't always forthcoming during our interview process. Browsing their pre-sentence reports allowed me to get a feel for the individuals and how they would cope within the prison system.

When I read the report on Malachi Donahue, I was perplexed as to how someone with his background could have ended up in prison. He strode into my office, a 6'4", 240-pound pecan-tanned, bald-headed stallion. No inmate ever made me feel uncomfortable, but Malachi had a commanding aura about him even though he never uttered a word.

I asked Malachi the usual questions for new commits, and he was curt with me as he rattled off his answers. He also took the liberty of advising me that he only had six months to do and he was in prison because he did "a favor for an old buddy," and that he had gotten rounded up with this bunch when they stopped in Atlanta to make some more drop-offs.

My response to him telling me that he was in prison because he did a favor for someone was, "Right—and I'm Diana Ross." If I had a nickel for every convict who insisted he was innocent, I would be rich. I informed him that I was his counselor for the duration of his stay at FPC-Williamsburg, and he needed to adhere to the rules and regulations of the facility or his stay might be extended beyond the six months.

Malachi looked at me arrogantly and said, "I don't think so, lady."

"You better watch your attitude," I told him. "I'm not the reason you're incarcerated. If you have a problem, you better take it up with the person that you claim is the cause of you being in jail."

CHAPTER 24

It wasn't unusual for inmates to do whatever they could to get under my skin. I could handle myself without being rude or obscene to anyone, but when Malachi was standing in the door to my office a week after his arrival, I couldn't help but get ready for another exchange of words. I immediately went on the defensive and asked, "What are you looking at, and what do you want?"

He held up in his arms in a gesture of surrender. "I just wondered if I could have a moment of your time."

I motioned my head for him to have a seat across from my desk. Malachi said, "Ms. Martin, I wanted to apologize for our first encounter. Since I've been here the other inmates have told me that you're pretty cool, and you go out of your way to help us as best you can. So I was told not to get on your bad side—otherwise, I might mess things up for everyone."

I said, "I'm glad that you all have nothing else better to do than talk about me like a bunch of little girls. I might suggest, Mr. Donahue that you find something else to do with your time other than inquire about me. Now is there anything else I can assist you with that pertains to your care and custody here at FPC-Williamsburg?"

He looked at me and said "No." I continued, "Well, good-bye then." He got up out of his seat and extended his hand in a truce for me to accept, but I just looked at him and said, "I don't think so, buddy."

He exited my office and I laughed to myself, except I didn't know that he hadn't walked away from my door. He poked his head back in my office and said, "I knew that you weren't as hard as you were pretending to be—I made you laugh."

I told him, "Mr. Donahue, I'm not laughing with you, I'm laughing at you."

He chuckled. "Ms. Martin that was a good one." Then he went back out into the unit.

I just shook my head, but I secretly admitted to myself that no inmate had ever made me feel as uneasy as Malachi Donahue did. Almost every day after the brief meeting in my office, I would look up and catch Malachi staring at me. I thought about telling his ass that stalking was a crime and he better find something else better to do with his time other than watch me.

But working in this type of atmosphere, you get used to men staring at you all the time. Hell, I'm one of the few females with whom they interact with until visiting day, and I'm not oblivious to them fantasizing about me. It got even worse when the administration disallowed them to have pornographic magazines. Now I don't know whose bright idea that was, but I would much prefer them whacking off to a fantasy girl in a magazine than stroking their johnson because they're daydreaming about me. This job is not for everybody—you always have to be thinking faster than the convicts because they are plotting and planning 24 hours a day, 7 days a week.

As much as Malachi Donahue made me uneasy, I had to be grateful for the one day that he was "stalking" me. I had an armload of papers that I had to organize for an inmate class project, and just as I left my office to head to the main building, a gust of wind blew them all over the outside field. I reacted before I could think about where I was. I put some of the papers on the ground and found a rock to hold them down. I was scurrying around trying to pick up the other papers that had blown all over the compound.

Behind me I heard an inmate say, "Face down, ass up—that's the way I like to fuck." Then I remembered where I was, and how I must have looked, down on the ground on my hands and knees with my ass in the air scrambling for papers. I got up and turned around to see an audience of inmates lined against the building who had been looking at me scamper around the yard like a fool. I couldn't identify the voice of the individual who'd just described his favorite sexual position, so I couldn't lash out at anyone.

Malachi Donahue walked up to me and said, "Here, Ms. Martin—I caught some of the papers that blew over by the unit." I snatched them out of his hands and he offered to help me carry the rest of the pile to my office in the main building. After my embarrassment, I didn't want to decline his offer, so I escorted him to the office.

Once there I unlocked the door, entered the office, and turned to say thank you to him. However, I didn't know that he'd been following me so closely, that's when I turned around and I bumped right into his chest and knocked the papers out of his hands. I felt like I had just run into a brick wall. Here I was again, with papers all over the floor.

We both knelt to pick up the papers, and that's when our hands touched. At that moment, I felt an electric current shoot up my hands to my head leaving me dizzy from his touch. I snatched my hand away from his and he jumped back to leave. But before he shut the door, he said "Ms. Martin, I heard what that guy said to you when you were on the ground outside, and that wasn't cool. I just want to apologize for someone talking to you like that."

I was at a loss for words. First of all, I was still trying to recover from the wooziness of touching his hand, and then I was in awe that an inmate was actually apologizing for something. I couldn't speak, so I just nodded my head.

CHAPTER 25

After the day I had at work, I needed a drink to relax my nerves. Before I knew it, I was sound asleep on my couch in front of the television. I awoke in a cold sweat, my heart beating so fast I thought it would burst through my chest. I couldn't shake the dream I'd just had: I was in my house, and I could feel the sensuous touch of a finger gliding down the spine of my back. Next, I could feel the hot kisses that teased my earlobes and neck. I was flipped over onto my back and I gasped for air as my nipples were suckled so tenderly, I just lay in bed immobilized by the trance I was in from my lover's obvious care for my body.

When I couldn't stand any more of the teasing, I arched my back with anticipation of our bodies merging as one. I spread my legs and welcomed entry into my warm center that was overflowing with my sweet juices, expressing my longing to be loved. I held on to my lover's strong body and anticipated his every stroke.

As he entered me, I exploded like a volcano because I couldn't contain the eruption. I cried and screamed at the burst of emotions that overflowed within me. My lover whispered in my ear, "Baby, now that I've found you, I will always make you feel this way, and I will protect you until the day that I die." Hearing those words made me smile and I felt at ease knowing that God had sent me just what I'd requested.

But when I opened my eyes, I saw Malachi Donahue staring me in the face. My dream had become a nightmare, and I felt as if I were committing a mortal sin.

I couldn't believe that our brief encounters would lead to such an erotic showdown. What the hell was wrong with me? I had to call Zondra. I was a little hesitant to tell her what had just happened, but I honestly wanted to relive the dream just to feel good.

When I told Zondra about my dream encounter, her response was, "Umm, you can't find anyone else to dream about?" I asked her what she thought my dream meant. She said, "It means you need to find another job, not to mention, you haven't had sex since you left Lance; it's just human nature to have those feelings—you're alright just as long as you don't act on them."

"I know that," I told her. "Besides, I've seen too many lonely people fall for inmates, both male and female, just to have it ruin their lives." I felt better talking to Zondra, at least I knew I was normal, and I didn't have to feel uneasy around Malachi Donahue while I was at work.

At work, I found myself working extra hard, especially since I was on a strategic mission to avoid Malachi. However, the more effort I put into trying to avoid him, the more I would run into him. He would come into my office to ask me questions when he could have easily gotten an answer from one of the other inmates. I entertained him just because I wanted to look at him; his mere presence was so smooth, and he had this air of confidence that made you think he didn't belong in prison. Our conversations were always casual, but there would always be a nervous feeling in the pit of my stomach when we were alone, and I couldn't think straight when he was around.

Regardless of how Malachi was making me feel, I had a job to do, and I couldn't fall prey to his wiles without the other inmates suspecting something. Instead of being in the housing unit with all of the inmates, I isolated myself in the main building where the inmates had very little access; they were only in the building if they were attending classes, visiting, or cleaning, or if they had been summoned by a staff member.

One day while I was in the main office filing paperwork away, I heard a knock at the door. I answered, "Come in" before I turned to see who was at the door. Malachi was standing there looking as tasty as a caramel square. I asked, "How may I help you, Mr. Donahue?"

Malachi responded, "May I ask you a question, Ms. Martin?"

I looked at him. "You walked all the way up here to ask me if you could ask me a question? Man, what do you really want?"

"If I tell you what I really wanted, you would send me to solitary confinement for the remainder of my stay here, and I don't want to be here if I can't see you every day." At that statement, my mouth got real dry. As he stepped toward me, I stood there frozen anticipating another opportunity to have him touch me.

However, another inmate knocked on the door, ending that brief exchange. It snapped me out of my trance and made Malachi pause. In a low voice, he said, "I'll talk to you later."

I had to get myself together, because this man was making me crazy. As much as I knew that it was wrong to think about him in a sexual way, everything I was feeling towards him felt so right. Therefore I was determined not to have any more "accidental" moments alone with him.

I was able to avoid him up until the time came for me to prepare his release packet. It had been five months since Malachi had come to the prison, and now that his stay was coming to an end, I had to sit down with him and review the plans for his supervision while he was on probation for the next year. I summoned Malachi to my office and inquired as to where he would reside and what his plans were for obtaining gainful employment. I was surprised when he told me that he had a job prior to his incarceration and he was going to continue in his family's real estate business; however, now that he'd visited South Carolina, he had a reason to expand his business ventures beyond Atlanta.

"That's a good idea," I told him. "The real estate market in South Carolina has really been booming since I arrived here." When I looked at him again, he licked his lips, and I almost fainted. In order to stay focused on the agenda at hand, I told him that he needed to be mindful of the friends that he hung around because now that he was a convicted felon, associating with less desirable individuals would be justification for his probation officer to write him up for a violation, and he would wind up right back in Salters occupying a bunk for the duration of his probation.

After I had Malachi sign all of his release paperwork, he said, "Ms. Martin, I've wanted to tell you something ever since I arrived here."

"And?" I asked.

"I know that with your job, you have a hard time trusting and believing everything an inmate says, but I was being honest when I said I was here because of someone I considered to be a friend. He left me holding the bag. I'm not saying I've been an angel all of my life, when I was in the game, I did my dirt, but I put all of that behind me. I'm a good man who works hard for my family and my future, and I don't want you to think that I'm like one of these knuckleheads around here with no aspirations."

I looked at Malachi. "Are you done with your confession?"

He laughed. "Ms. Martin, you're funny. I like that about you." I was speechless. He continued, "I'm not interested in South Carolina just for its real estate prospects—I'm coming back here to win you over. I know that this is your job, and I wouldn't want to do anything that would cause you to lose it, but once I get out of here, it's all fair game. I like your style, your walk, and your way of handling yourself around these clowns, so I'm gonna come back for you."

I must have looked astonished. He went on, "Just like me, I know that you felt something between us the day I helped you with those papers. Since then, I can't get you out of my head. I always get what I want, Ms. Martin, and my plan for the future is to make you mine."

Any other time, I would have had a snappy comeback for Mr. Donahue, but I couldn't think of a reply for anything that I just heard. All I was able to get out of my mouth was, "Well, Mr. Donahue, I wish you well in your future endeavors, but you can get your mind off of me because it's not going to happen."

"We'll see about that, Ms. Martin," he said before he left.

Lord, I couldn't wait until this man's release date came and went so I could get myself together. His mere presence was throwing me off track, and I couldn't function right as long as he was around.

CHAPTER 26

Malachi Donahue's release date was rapidly approaching. I'd been able to avoid him during the last month of his sentence, and I was relieved he was finally departing. But just before he left the camp, he poked his head in my office door and said, "I'll be back, Ms. Martin."

I replied, "I'll have a bunk waiting for you." He laughed and went out of the building with a horde of other inmates following behind him wishing him well. I was happy that he was gone, now I could do my job without so many distractions. His absence allowed me to forget our brief encounters and how they made me feel.

It was close to six months after Malachi's release date that he made good on his promise. I considered him a distant memory until I received a letter at my home without a return address. Inside the envelope was a three-page letter that began by advising me not to be alarmed by its contents. I read the letter in its entirety and learned that Malachi had used the Internet to locate me. He didn't want to just show up on my doorstep and frighten me to death, so he was sending this letter to express how he felt about me.

I could have fallen out on the floor, but the words in his letter captivated me, and no matter how I tried, I couldn't put the papers down. Malachi wrote that he was impressed with me as a woman who had to work with hardened criminals on a daily basis, yet I was still professional on all levels without being disrespectful or demeaning to them like so many other staff members often were. He said he had thought about me every day since we'd accidentally touched hands. He added that he knew he couldn't pursue me in the situation that he was in then, but now that things had changed, he couldn't live with himself if he never uttered a word as to how he felt about me. He wanted me to know he was impressed with me as a person, and he was turned on by the way I smiled, smelled, walked, and talked.

I had to blush at his words, it had been so long since I had a man compliment me in any way, but his words were pure and genuine, and this was what I really needed at the moment. But as soon as I finished reading his letter, reality set in. I had to come to grips with the idea that this was a former inmate who'd tracked me down and wrote me a damn letter confessing his feelings towards me.

All of this was too much for me to absorb, and I immediately thought the letter I was holding crossed the line when it came to professional ethics. How could I ever explain to anyone that I was interested in a former inmate?

Malachi had ended his letter by saying he was going to be in town for business reasons and he wanted to meet me for dinner. He noted his personal information in his letter so I could get in contact with him to let him know my answer.

I thought long and hard about responding to Malachi's letter because I didn't know what to expect, then against my better judgment, I got on the phone and dialed the number from the letter.

Malachi picked up on the second ring. "Hello."

I've never been at a lost for words, but at that instant, my mouth was open but no words were escaping my lips, I was so nervous, it took everything in me just to mumble "Hi".

"Ms. Martin, is that you?"

I chuckled and suddenly felt comfortable. "Listen, you don't have to call me Ms. Martin any longer."

He laughed and said, "I'm sorry—it's just that I'm shocked to hear from you."

I asked Malachi what he was thinking by sending me a letter. He indicated he'd meant every word of it, and he'd been kicking himself every day after his departure because he'd allowed so much time to lapse before he built up enough nerve to contact me and express how he felt.

Our conversation was getting intense, and I had to put him on hold just to process everything he was saying. I asked, "How could you become so enamored with me just by watching me do my job?"

Instead of answering, he said, "Denise, I wrote you that letter explaining just how I felt. Now that you've had the opportunity to read it, I would like to take you out to dinner, and we can discuss anything you want to."

My mind was racing at his request, and I told him I would have to think about it. He said, "I promise you won't regret going out with me, because I'm a true gentleman. I just want to really show you what I'm all about." Malachi indicated he didn't want to pressure me, so he would let me make the decision on my own. He told me that he would be in town over the weekend, and if I wanted to see him I could meet him at the local shopping mall since it was neutral ground, and we could determine what to do from there.

I said, "I don't think meeting at the mall is a good idea, because people I work with also live in this town, and I can't risk the chance of someone recognizing you and then reporting me to the administrative staff." He protested that he was no longer an inmate and he wouldn't be treated like one. I indicated that I understood how he felt, but if he wanted to see me, it was going to be on my terms only. With that being said, Malachi told me to make the plans and let him know the arrangements. Before I could think things through clearly, I told him that the only place I would feel comfortable would be in the privacy of my own home. Therefore, I would make dinner for us and we could talk without me being paranoid about someone I knew seeing us.

Malachi asked, "Are you sure?"

"Yes. I'll expect you at seven-thirty this Friday. And since you went through the trouble of looking up my personal information on the Internet, you can download directions to my home the same way."

He laughed. "Woman, you know that was the first thing I did when I found out where you were."

I said, "I'll see you on Friday, Malachi," and I smiled as I hung up the telephone. I then tried calling called Zondra, but only got her voicemail, so I left her a message to call me back.

In the meantime, I had to think about what I'd just done. In my line of work, I've witnessed several relationships blossom between staff and inmates. Sometimes it happened when inmates were still serving their sentence, and others grew into something after an inmate was released. Those who got caught having an intimate relationship with an inmate were immediately fired, and most were charged with sexual abuse. The BOP's stance on inmate and staff personal relationships was firm: it is viewed as an abuse of authority if a staff member is caught having a relationship with an inmate, and it also restricts contact with a former inmate for one year after their release. I was weighing all the pros and cons of inviting Malachi into my humble abode, but I had a nagging feeling that I would undoubtedly regret it if I didn't throw caution to the wind and just listen to what he had to say.

It was close to midnight when Zondra finally returned my call. She said that she'd been busy working on some business ventures outside of practicing law. I told her that I had a 911 emergency and needed her to be my voice of reason. She listened intently and analyzed every word I said before advising me that I wasn't breaking any laws by having dinner with Malachi, especially since he was no longer an inmate. "But where do you really expect things to go after that?" she asked.

I told her that I really didn't know, and I hadn't thought that far ahead. "Maybe you should," she replied, "because going to the company picnic with a former inmate is not going to be a good look for you."

As much as I hated to admit it, Zondra was right, but I had to experience life for myself. I told her I was going to live in the moment without analyzing everything; this was just one date that might not lead to another. She'd offered her words of wisdom as both a friend and an attorney, and I thanked her for not being judgmental towards me.

"You and Malachi are two single adults simply having dinner. You've done nothing that would cause me or anyone else to pass judgment on you," she said. "But as soon as he leaves on Friday, I want a telephone call with all the juicy details."

Zondra was right: we were just having dinner together. I was single and so was he. Besides it wasn't as if I were going to marry the man—I was just going to make him something to eat and find out why he was so intrigued by me.

CHAPTER 27

The week went by so fast. By the time Friday rolled around, I was a nervous wreck, wondering if inviting Malachi to my house was a huge mistake. I had so much to do in preparation for his arrival. I cooked, cleaned the house, and lit the scented candles, but then I couldn't decide on what to wear. I finally chose a pair of comfortable jeans and a backless tunic top. My hair was shampooed and cascaded down my back so I thought he would be impressed with how I looked. I was nervous and I didn't know why, since I wasn't expecting too much from our conversation. I just wanted to hear what Malachi had to say and why he thought he was the man for me.

Malachi was very punctual, arriving at 7:30 on the dot. Before I answered the door, I said a silent prayer to God: "Lord, I don't know how or why I'm doing this but I'm walking out on faith, trusting that you will guide me in the right direction." God must have heard my cry because when I opened the door and saw Malachi standing there with a bouquet of flowers in his hand, I got weak in the knees. I could smell his cologne from the small breeze of the night air—it was simply intoxicating.

I asked him to come in and have a seat while I finished preparing dinner. Malachi asked if I wanted him to do anything. I told him that as he was a guest in my home, I would cater to him for now. Then I told him that he was welcome to relax on the couch while I talked to him from the kitchen. I revealed our menu for the night, and he said he hadn't eaten anything all day long because he was so excited about this evening.

Once I'd set the table, I invited Malachi to have a seat. He started laughing, and I thought I'd done something terribly wrong. He asked, "Are you cooking for some other guests, because there's no way that I can eat all of this food?" I looked at the table and had to laugh also. I had grilled steak, chicken, and fried shrimp. Then I'd made loaded baked potatoes, house salad, and steamed vegetables. I told Malachi that as I wasn't sure about what he liked to eat, so I had cooked a little of everything.

"You did a good job," he said. "Everything looks wonderful."

Once we were seated, Malachi shocked me when he asked if he could bless the food. I smiled and before bowing my head, I gave God a wink and told him *thank you.*

Dinner was great and conversation with Malachi was easy. He told me all about his childhood and growing up in Atlanta. Apparently he had a twin brother named Malcolm with whom he was extremely close. His parents were active in the community, and before he went to prison, he'd been working on purchasing, renovating, and reselling homes in the Atlanta area.

"Everyone seems to be in the house-flipping business these days," I told him.

"That's true, but I'm different. I do most of the repairs and renovations myself. Anything that's too complicated—I have lots of contacts so I can find people to help me get things done without ripping me off."

"You know, looking at you I would have never have thought you were so well established."

"Yeah, I know you really couldn't tell too much about me from the prison uniform I was wearing." Then he got serious and said, "Denise, I knew you felt something between us the day our hands touched. I know that it's not by accident or chance that I met you. Even though I would have preferred meeting you under different circumstances and I know what kind of situation this may put you in, and I don't want to jeopardize your future. So I understand why you didn't want to go out with me," especially since you didn't know my intentions."

I just kept looking at him as he continued, "But, Denise Martin, I want you to know that I've wasted enough of my time hanging with the wrong crowd and dating the wrong women. My time in prison helped me to redirect my focus in life. I'm not playing any games with you, and me being here should prove to you that I'm serious about what I want out of life. I've been given another chance, and I'm going to do things the right way now."

As Malachi was being so honest with me, I had to let him know what was going through my mind. We finished up with dinner and moved to my couch as I told him about my marriage to Lance and my previous relationship with Carl. He listened to everything I had to say about how much heartache I'd experienced when I thought I was in love. I expressed to him that I'd been cheated on in relationships that I thought were solid and trust was a big issue with me.

Malachi continued to listen intently as I spoke about my past loves, telling him, "Look, all I'm trying to say is, when I'm in a committed relationship, my mate doesn't have to worry about me cheating or playing any games with him, but it seems as if I'm always the one being cheated on and getting her heart broken. I just want to be secure in knowing that I can turn my back and my man won't be chasing the first short skirt he sees. I've been let down before, and I'm just not ready to go down that road again, so if I happen to come across as abrasive or harsh, then it's just me putting my guard up against getting hurt again."

He nodded his head. "I can understand your reasons for not trusting, but why are you letting what those jerks did to you make you hate all men? Denise, I can't fault you for feeling the way that you do, but I know me, and I know how to treat a lady. If you allow me into your life, I promise you that I can make you forget all the pain and embarrassment your ex-husband and ex-boyfriend caused you."

I looked at him and told him, "My heart says to believe you, but my head is telling me not to trust anything that you are saying."

"Look, if you allow fear to stop you from experiencing life, then you've let everyone who has hurt you control your life and destiny—you've decided to let someone else steal your joy." He was right: I had to let the past go in order to move on.

Malachi held my chin up, looked me in my eyes, and said "Do what your heart is telling you to do, Denise." Before I knew it, we were kissing so passionately, and I was locked in an embrace from which I couldn't withdraw. When Malachi picked me up off of the couch, I was swept away by the scent of him. It was as if he had a spell over me.

While he carried me, he asked for directions to my bedroom. I couldn't speak, so I just pointed in the direction I wanted him to go. "Do you want me to make love to you?" he asked gently.

"I haven't ever wanted anything as badly as I want you at this moment."

After we entered my bedroom, Malachi gently placed me on the bed. He tenderly removed my pants and untied my top. I lay on my bed completely naked; spreading my legs to let him see what could be his. It was as if I was reliving my dream.

Malachi stripped out of his clothes, and it was apparent he took care of his body. He had washboard abs, and his skin was smooth rather than rough as I would expect of someone who renovated homes. His chest was big and hard from doing so much carpentry work. As I watched him, it felt as though my dream had come true.

Before he climbed into my bed, he removed a condom from his pants pocket and put it on the nightstand. I said, "Hey, you come prepared." He just smiled and began kissing my hands, working his way all the way down to my feet. Everything was so perfect with Malachi that I thought for sure this moment was only a figment of my imagination. But I knew my fantasy was real when he slipped on the condom and entered me, and I just shuddered at the wave of emotions that enveloped me.

Malachi talked to me as he made love to me, saying "Denise, I've been thinking about this moment for a long time, and now that I'm here I'm going to make you happy as long as you let me." I'd been holding onto Malachi for dear life when he spoke those words, and it was as if that was what I needed to hear. I fell into an orgasmic bliss that had me screaming and crying from pleasure.

As Malachi reached his own climax, he said, "Baby, you can let it all out. I'm here now, and I plan to be a part of your life for a long time to come." This moment was amazing—having Malachi next to me felt dangerous, and yet so right. I could talk to him as if I had known him all of my life, and he was so gentle as we made love. Even if this was a mistake, I was glad I'd taken this chance.

We fell asleep in each other's arms, I prayed and asked God to guide me in the right direction. *Please don't let sleeping with this man be a mistake because I haven't felt this safe and secure in a very long time.*

It was two o'clock in the morning when I heard the telephone ringing. It was Zondra calling to see how my date with Malachi had gone. I whispered as to not wake Malachi, telling her I was still on the date but I promised to call her later in the day with all of the details. She said "tramp" laughingly before I hung up the phone.

Malachi said, "I'm not sleep—I heard you."

"Well, since you're up, let's make the best of this moment." I climbed on top of Malachi and rode him until his toes curled from my skills. He responded as if we were lovers reuniting after some time apart. It had been so long since someone had made me feel so good. I knew my life would not be the same after I made love to Malachi, but I couldn't have cared less about what others thought about me or how it came to be that we were united. My first night with him was the beginning of something special, and I planned to hold him to his promises.

CHAPTER 28

True to his word, during the ten months we'd been dating, Malachi had done everything in his power to make me the happiest woman alive. Our visits were generally on the weekend, and they were over too soon. He frequently visited South Carolina when he could and I was in Atlanta every time I had a break. Malachi and I were doing our best to make this long distance relationship last.

I knew that our relationship was changing as soon as Malachi suggested that I meet his family. Plans for the Donahue Family Reunion were under way, and Malachi thought it would be the perfect time to introduce me to everyone. I was a little skeptical at first. I mean, meeting the parents is one thing, but meeting an entire family is a whole different scenario. I was unsure as to what they would think about me; after all I did meet Malachi while he was in prison. Malachi assured me that know one would be thinking about that, his incarceration was in the past, and no one is looking back. "We're only looking ahead to the future," he said.

When that man put everything in perspective, how could I say no to him? I really fell in love with the Donahue family. It was easy to see that they were a close-knit group, and inviting towards anyone who entered their home. His parents, Patrick and Michelle Donahue, and his brother Malcolm were very receptive of me, even after Malachi and I divulged how we met. They just laughed and said it didn't matter how—as long as we made each other happy, they were fine with us being together.

Malachi and his Malcolm were mirror images of one another. The only difference was that Malachi was slightly taller and more muscular than Malcolm. To see them together made me realize what a bond they must share, and I hoped that my nephews Keith and Kelby were this close when they grew up.

As for Mr. and Mrs. Donahue, they were delightful. It was obvious they were proud of their sons and supported them in every aspect of their lives. What Malachi had neglected to tell me was that not only were his parents prominent real estate investors, they were moguls. They'd built a profitable business that catered to an array of notable clientele throughout the metropolitan Atlanta area. I was impressed and proud that Malachi had come from such great lineage.

With the family reunion taking place in Atlanta, I thought this would also be the perfect opportunity for Malachi to meet my dear friend Zondra, besides having her with me made me feel a little more comfortable about being surrounded by so many of Malachi's family members. It was important for Zondra to meet Malachi because her opinion was very important to me, and now that he was in my life, I had to introduce him to her.

Zondra met me at Malachi's parents' home where they were having a barbecue for the family. I introduced her to everyone, and while Malachi was talking to his parents and brother, she and I slipped away into the house. I wanted to get her honest opinion about Malachi. She just hugged me and said, "Girl, if he makes you smile as much as you've been smiling, then it shouldn't matter what I think about him. Obviously he has your heart, Denise, and you would be a fool to let him go."

I hugged Zondra and thanked her for being in my life. She said, "Now let's work on that brother of his for me." I told her no problem. Zondra couldn't believe she'd been in Atlanta for almost eight years without ever running into Malcolm. I told her everything happens in God's timing, so she had to be patient and trust that God would bring the perfect man into her life. Then hopefully she would find the same kind of happiness I had with Malachi.

Malachi had showed me how much he cared about me by introducing me to his family, and they accepted me with open arms. Now, I had to reciprocate the favor and let him meet the Martin crew. My family was not like Malachi's, but he was now a part of my life, I had to let him in completely without fearing what others may think about us.

Thanksgiving was coming up, and I made arrangements to take Malachi home to Miami and introduce him to my family. Once I made the announcement to my family that I was bringing a guest home for Thanksgiving, my mother had a zillion questions for me, but I told her we would talk in depth once I made it home.

I've never been as nervous as I was by the time Malachi and I drove from South Carolina to Miami. He kept rubbing my hand, reassuring me that things would be alright. I smiled at his support, but he didn't know my mother.

When we arrived at my parents' home, everyone rushed out to greet me. It had been over a year since I'd been home and I'd really missed my silly sisters. My nephews were getting so big, and my mom and dad looked good as well.

I ran up to Pops and hugged him. He said, "My baby girl made it back home. How are you doing, darling?"

"Fine, Daddy—and I brought my boyfriend for you all to meet."

After all the hugs and kisses were over, everyone went inside the house to settle down. Deb and Diane said, "Denise, he is cute—how come you never said anything about him before today?" I told them that I wasn't too sure if they would approve of our relationship if they knew how we had met. But then I changed the subject. Deborah was four months pregnant, so we talked about her due date and what she was having.

Malachi was in the family room with Pops, Deb's husband Kevin, and Diane's boyfriend David. They were watching football and making a ruckus. My mom was in the kitchen finishing the dinner preparations. It was great to be back home with my sisters.

While we were busy chatting, my mom called from the kitchen: "Ya'll don't have no maid around here. Instead of bumping ya'll gums, you could be doing something useful like setting the dining table for dinner."

My sisters and I just looked at each other and burst out laughing. I said, "It's funny how some things never change."

Once we'd set the dishes on the table, we placed the food out, and before Mom could announce that dinner was ready, the men were racing into the dining room to find a seat, claiming we were torturing them with the aromas. The sight of these grown men jockeying for a seat that would allow for adequate elbow space was hilarious. My nephews were big as hell now and required seating at the adult table since they had outgrown the children's table.

When everyone had settled down and before we got ready to dig into the meal, Pops asked everyone to bow their heads for a prayer. He said, "Lord, I would like to thank you for all of your blessings. I want to thank you for protecting my children and grandchildren. I also want to thank you for these young men who are in the lives of my girls. Help them to be the men you created them to be. And finally, I want to thank you for my wife because without her, none of us would be here."

After Pops was finished, we all said amen, then began passing the bowls of food around the table, piling the food high on our plates, while Pops carved the turkey. My sisters and I fussed at him for testing the meat before we had a chance to get our select pieces. As annoying as my family can be, I missed having them around, especially on special occasions such as this one.

We were all enjoying dinner and having a great time until my mentally challenged sister Diane opened her big mouth and said, "So Niecey, tell us how you and Malachi met."

I looked at Malachi and he looked at me, because he didn't know I hadn't told my family all about us. I gulped really hard and said, "I had met him at work," thinking that this answer would be good enough for the meantime.

But noooo, Diane just wouldn't let it go at that. She asked Malachi, "What's your job in the prison?"

Malachi looked at her and said, "I don't work in the prison—I used to live there." At that announcement, everyone stopped eating and turned in my direction. I was put on the spot and couldn't stand the pressure. Not wanting to face my family when they were giving me this kind of scrutiny, I got up and ran to the bathroom.

My sister Deborah came after me, apologizing for Diane. "We had no idea how you and Malachi met. I'm sorry we intruded on your privacy." I let Deb in the bathroom and told her that I was sorry, but I didn't want anyone to pass judgment on Malachi without knowing him because he was a great man.

She said, "Well if he's so great, don't run away. Go and stand by your man." After listening to Deborah, I dried up my tears and went out to face my family and apologize to Malachi.

When I walked out to the dining room, I told everyone I had an announcement to make. I explained that Malachi and I had met while he was serving a six-month sentence at the prison where I currently worked, but our relationship didn't evolve until after he'd been released. I told them, "I've been with him for ten months now, and I'm in love with him."

Once I confirmed my love for Malachi, he stood up and said, "I love you too, baby." Then he got down on one knee in front of me and said, "Mr. and Mrs. Martin, I have been in love with your daughter from the moment I first saw her, and I would like to have your permission for her hand in marriage." He pulled a black box out of his pants pocket and asked, "Denise, would you be my wife?"

But before I could answer Malachi, my mother immediately said, "No! There's no way my daughter will marry an ex-convict."

I looked at my big sister and she nodded her head at me and smiled. "Mom," I said. "That's not your decision to make." Then I looked Malachi in the eyes and told him, "I would love to be your wife." My mom stormed out of the room but Pops came over to shake Malachi's hand and hug me.

There was no need for dessert after that major production, and besides my mother was carrying on like someone had stolen her favorite pearls. Diane and Deb told the men to go back into the family room to watch television and they complied like obedient animals. I guess no one knew what to say or do after I'd let the cat out of the bag. My sisters and I just hugged, and they kept asking me, "Does he make you happy?" I told them of course he did.

But then Diane with her ignorant ass went straight for the jugular by saying, "Look since he's been in jail and all, are you sure that he's not gay?"

"There is no way in the world that a man who makes love like Malachi could be gay. You watch too much television." Deb told me not to listen to Diane because she didn't know what real love is. Diane gave Deb and me the middle finger, then left the kitchen. My big sister just hugged me without saying a word.

Malachi's meeting my family was definitely a Thanksgiving to remember. Although Pops pleaded with me to stay at the house, I decided it would be best if Malachi and I rented a hotel room for the remainder of our stay in Miami. We had so much to talk about now that we were engaged. I couldn't believe how my heart swelled with emotions because he still wanted to marry me despite how simple my mom acted.

After Malachi and I made it to the hotel, I had a chance to think things through rationally. When we were in our room, I asked Malachi, "Are you sure you want to marry me?"

"I wouldn't have asked, if I wasn't sure."

I hugged him so tightly and told him I was sorry I'd never mentioned his prison term to my family.

"It doesn't matter. What does matter is the way you stood up for me. It made me so proud, and I knew then that we could face anything together."

However, reality began to set in. "What about my job?" I asked him.

Malachi just smiled at me. "You're my woman, and I plan on taking care of you for the rest of your life, so you can quit your job and join the family business, or you can be a housewife and raise all of my babies."

At that, I laughed at Malachi and said, "Well Mr. Donahue, we have some decisions to make, but first let's call your parents and give them the news."

His parents were elated at our announcement. Mrs. Donahue started crying and said, "I'm glad you're going to be my daughter-in-law. Now I don't have to be the only female with my rowdy bunch of men."

When the phone call ended, Malachi and I celebrated our engagement by ordering champagne and toasting to our future together. We ended the night by making love and vowing to never let anything or anyone come between us. I had found love again, and he'd showed me that I could trust once more. I would not let anything or anyone destroy my future with this man.

CHAPTER 29

Before Malachi and I left Miami, I had to tell my parents good-bye, so we went by the house before we got on the road. My mother was still upset about my pending nuptials, but I had no idea she would show total disrespect towards Malachi and disregard my feelings for the man I intended to marry. While we were at the house, she said she'd invited a guest over and didn't want me to leave before that person had arrived.

I was in the family room with Malachi and Pops watching television when I heard the doorbell ring, I went to go answer the door, and somebody could have knocked me over with a feather because standing in front of me, big and bold, was Lance.

I wanted to slam the door in his face, but he put his foot against it and said, "Could I come in, Denise? It's been a long time, and I think you should know about some things that have gone on since we parted ways."

I was livid to say the least. My mom had planned this entire scene, and I was boiling hot right about now. But then just as I was standing at the door talking to Lance, Malachi appeared and asked "Baby, is everything alright?" I turned to face Malachi and introduced him to Lance. Malachi said, "I will leave you two alone so you all can talk."

"Don't leave the room," I told him. "Anything Lance had to say to me, he can say in front of you as well."

Lance said, "Alright, if that's how you want it, I came here today with the hopes of us getting back together. I know that this Malachi is your new boyfriend, but Denise—things between us ended the wrong way. That whole thing with Rebecca was a mistake. She was out to hurt you all along. For reasons unknown to me, that woman has tried her best to tarnish my reputation, especially since I wouldn't commit to a relationship with her."

"What about the baby?" I asked.

"Rebecca was never pregnant by me. She was having an affair with my assistant, and it was his baby. When he wouldn't leave his wife for her, she decided to set me up. Now Denise, I'm not saying I wasn't at fault for the night you walked in on us, but I want to sincerely apologize for breaking your heart and ruining our marriage."

When Lance finished his declaration, I looked him straight in the eye and said, "I accept your apology, and I forgive you for what you did to us, but as far as us getting back together, it won't happen in this lifetime." I showed him the three-carat ring that Malachi had given to me the previous night. "This man standing right here next to me is who I want to build my future with. He showed me how to love again, and I trust him with everything—something I would never be able to do with you."

My parents were standing in the foyer by this time, and I turned around and told Mom, "If you want to lose a daughter, then keep trying to interfere with my decisions."

Lance spoke up again, "I know you can't be serious about this convict."

I could feel the heat rise up to my head as I turned around and told Lance that Malachi was more man than he would ever be, I was livid, and if I had stayed in my parents' home any longer, I think my mom and I would have been reenacting the "Thriller in Manila" boxing match right there in her own home. I stormed out of the house with Malachi on my heels and we drove all the way back to South Carolina in complete silence.

When we arrived at my home, Malachi walked me inside and said he didn't want to cause any trouble with me and my family, so if I wanted to reconsider his proposal, he would understand. I cried in his arms and told him if I had to choose, then I chose him. Tomorrow I would be putting in my resignation for my job and I would start preparing for our wedding.

Malachi picked me up. "Baby, I promise I will spend the rest of my life making you happy."

I told him, "I didn't think it was possible, but you've already made me happier than I've ever been."

CHAPTER 30

Once I calmed down and could think a little more clearly, Malachi told me to hold off on turning in my letter of resignation at least until we got married. We had a wedding to plan, and he didn't want me to make any rash decisions without thinking everything through. He told me to let him get things straight in Atlanta, and he would come back on the weekends to assist me with our wedding preparations and packing up my personal belongings.

I wanted to get married as soon as possible, but having a courthouse wedding was out of the question with Malachi. He said that this was going to be the most memorable day of his life, and he wanted all of our loved ones to witness our union as he professed his commitment to me. This man was too good to be true, and I was overjoyed that he wanted to be with me. We decided to get married next July. It was eight months away, but I had to get rolling because there were so many decisions to make and it didn't look as if I would have too much help from my mother.

The reality of planning a wedding had me overwhelmed, and the fact Malachi wasn't there every day only intensified my anxiety and I felt like I was all alone. One evening when I was feeling real lonely, Malachi called to talk to me, but when he tried to discuss the wedding, I just started crying hysterically. He tried to console me by saying, "Baby, everything is fine. I love you, and you love me. Nothing has changed—you're just upset because I'm not there right now, but trust that I'm in Atlanta trying to make a home for us, something that you'll love."

I said, "OK." Malachi knew how I was feeling, and I didn't want him to think I was having second thoughts about being his wife.

To calm my worries, Malachi suggested "Baby, go get your Bible. I want to read something to you."

After I had it in my hands, I asked Malachi what book he wanted me to turn to. He said, "Philippians four, verses six and seven. Read it with me."

Don't worry about anything; instead pray, about everything. Tell God what you need, and thank him for all he has done. If you do this, you will experience God's peace, which is far more wonderful than the human mind can understand. His peace will guard your hearts and minds as you live in Christ Jesus.

"Thank you for that, sweetheart," I told him. "I really needed to hear that, and I'm glad you knew just what to do."

"Baby, I got your back. I told you we're in this thing together."

When I got off of the phone with my man, I was at peace. I started reading my Bible more, and one day a slip of paper fell out. I unfolded the paper and I smiled when I saw the list that I wrote when I had requested from God to send me a man with the following qualities:

Loves the Lord

Has a J-O-B

Someone I can *trust*

Does not have any children (*no baby mama drama*)

Respects his mother

He *loves* me unconditionally

Handsome

Tall

Romantic

Can tolerate my family

After looking at the list I'd had made for God, I knew that no matter how difficult I thought things were, he was in the midst of it, and that as long as I trusted in him, everything would work out fine. Having that list fall out of my Bible was God's way of confirming that Malachi was the one for me.

CHAPTER 31

While Malachi made preparations for our life in Atlanta, I submerged myself in the preparations for our wedding. We were going to be married in the church in which Malachi grew up. I had to coordinate much of the wedding through Zondra; she was in Atlanta and could get a lot of my legwork done for me. She was also my maid of honor, and it was her duty to assist me in any way that I saw fit. My sisters were going to be my bridesmaids, and Deb was going to do everyone's hair in the bridal party.

Even my mom had seemed to come around and tried to assist me with planning my reception. She apologized for the way she'd reacted to Malachi during Thanksgiving. I told her to just give him a chance. If she knew how determined he was to make me just as happy as Daddy had made her during their marriage, she wouldn't have to worry about whether I was making the right decision.

Mom said, "I just want the best for you girls, and I don't see how he's the best thing for you."

"I'm not going to get into a debate with you about my decision to marry Malachi. If you want to support me, then show up at the church at the scheduled time. Otherwise, I don't want to hear another word about what you think is best for me."

After I told her how I felt, she said, "I understand" and hung up the telephone. Malachi and I had come such a long way that I wasn't going to let my own mother spoil this moment for me.

Malachi and I planned on renting out my townhouse until we felt the market was right to sell it. Since he was the expert in that area, I agreed with him. I had already turned in my resignation letter at work, which meant that was one less thing I had to worry about. But, between making wedding preparations, packing up my house, and making time for Malachi, I was exhausted by the time my wedding date approached. Yet even with everything I'd been through, I couldn't wait to walk down the aisle and stand next to Malachi.

CHAPTER 32

My wedding was only two days away, and all I had to do was get through the wedding rehearsal and down the aisle to Malachi. Everyone was on time, and even my mother looked as if she were excited for me. Reverend Kendrick Patterson was going to be the officiating minister for the day. He was Malachi's pastor, and he needed to make sure that Malachi and I were making the right decision as far as God was concerned. Therefore we'd had to take premarital classes that helped us to really understand our roles as husband and wife. After eight sessions, I was convinced that God had given his permission for me to marry this man.

Getting everyone to Georgia for the wedding rehearsal had been no small feat. I had to persuade my parents to leave the comforts of their home for a few days. Zondra was willing to accommodate me and my entire family as we prepared for my wedding. Having the family under one roof eased any anxieties my parents were having about the upcoming event, plus knowing that all of her girls were in one place made my mom feel more comfortable.

Reverend Patterson went through the processional, and it was over. My wedding rehearsal had been perfect. Now it was time for everyone to dine at the Olive Garden, which was one of my favorite places to eat. We all had a good time, and Pops gave a toast to me and Malachi. Once he got everyone's attention, he said, "Malachi, first I would like to thank your parents for raising a good man. You have put a smile on my daughter's face that brightens up the room when she enters. I wish nothing but the best for you all, and all of my grandbabies that you are going to give to us. Welcome to the family, son!"

Everyone cracked up laughing at the toast and I knew that this is what love felt like. Then Malachi's brother, who was the best man, took the opportunity to clang his glass because he also wanted to say a few words about his brother. Malcolm stood up and said, "I want to let everyone know how proud I am of my big brother, who's older by two minutes. He got through a tough six months in his life and he came out with a lovely woman by his side, who introduced me to the woman I'm in love with. I just want to tell my brother and Denise congratulations and let them know that they really inspire me to be a better person."

Malachi stood up and walked over to his brother, then hugged him. Seeing them be so affectionate towards one another made me smile, and I looked over at Zondra and winked my eye at her. Since I'd introduced her to Malcolm at the Donahue's barbecue, they'd been joined at the hip. I reminded Zondra that all she used to have time for was her job, but now that Malcolm had come into her life, her nose was wide open, and she didn't even have time for her best friend anymore. She just laughed and said, "Girl, that man is like a breath of fresh air, and I plan on taking him all in for as long as he lets me."

I said, "Alright, Ms. Hill, do your thang, girl, I know that you already put your whip appeal on that man. That's why he's standing up in a room full of strangers confessing his love for you."

Zondra laughed again. "Yeah, he is acting sprung, huh." We both laughed as if we were the only ones in on the joke.

Once dinner was over with, Malachi and I thanked everyone for coming and reminded them that they better be on time tomorrow because the wedding would start promptly, with or without them. I told Malachi he could go out with his friends, but to make sure he called me when he got in because I wanted his voice to be the last thing I heard before I went to sleep.

Meanwhile, I was going to stay up with my sisters and Zondra. I was a nervous wreck, and I kept going over the itinerary for my wedding with the girls. I insisted that Deb finish everyone's hair that night because everything had to be perfect. Besides, she didn't have time to be fussing with anyone's hair tomorrow except for mine. I spent the majority of the night double-checking everything until Zondra and my sisters accused me of both being a party pooper and turning into a Bridezilla. They went to their rooms to get some sleep, but I couldn't go to sleep until I heard Malachi's voice to know that he was alright.

Just before I got ready to call him on his cell phone, Zondra told me I had a call, and I could take it in her study room for some privacy. When I picked up the receiver, I wasn't surprised to hear Malachi's voice say, "Hey pretty lady, are you ready to be my wife?"

I told him, "You just meet me at the church tomorrow and wait to see what my answer will be."

"I love you, Denise Martin. If someone had told me a year-and-a-half ago that I would be getting married to the correctional counselor who worked at the prison I served time in, I'd have thought they were playing a cruel joke on me. But darling, this is real, and what I feel for you is real. I'm so glad God put you in my life."

"You're going to make me cry if you don't stop with all of those mushy words."

"Alright, baby, I'll just see you tomorrow. Make sure you get enough rest because I'm going to make sure that you don't sleep at all after I make you my wife."

I said, "Goodnight, Mr. Donahue, I love you. Make sure you dream of only me."

CHAPTER 33

The morning of my wedding day was perfect. I got up and went walking with Zondra just to get the jitters out of my stomach. We returned to her home where my mom had prepared a lavish breakfast. After we ate, we all went to our rooms to prepare for the day's big event.

Deborah was waiting in my room after I got out of the shower, she still had to style my hair. Diane was being a dutiful bridesmaid as well, making sure all of the other ladies in the bridal party were on point. It was like she'd turned into a drill sergeant overnight. I was proud of my baby sister, who had grown up from being the brat I was so used to. Now she was a top hair and makeup model who'd been requested to host fashion shows all over the world just like the model commentator for *Jet*, Jada Collins. It appeared all of those visits to Deb's salon had paid off after all. Parlaying her good features and brains with her business degree that she received from Florida International University, Diane had even managed to keep a steady boyfriend who wasn't intimidated by her alluring features.

By noon everyone had to be dressed and downstairs waiting for the limousine that would drive us to the church. All I could think about was seeing my soon-to-be husband and imagining his face as he watched me walk down the aisle toward him and our future together. Deborah pulled my hair up so that Malachi would see my face after my daddy lifted my veil. Thanks to the precise application by Diane, my makeup was flawless; even the photographer said I was the most beautiful bride he'd ever captured. I said a silent prayer to God because this day had finally arrived, and so far it was better than I could have ever imagined. All I had to do was exchange vows with Malachi, then hear the preacher pronounce us as husband and wife.

The church decorations were lovely. I couldn't have asked for anything better, Zondra and my sisters had done a fabulous job with my colors of crimson and cream. This day was special, and I was so glad Malachi had persuaded me to have a traditional wedding instead of a drive-through version at the courthouse.

With everyone in place, I was ready to go as soon as I heard "Here Comes the Bride." I had my daddy by my side, and he kissed my hand and said, "Baby girl, I am so proud of you. I hope Malachi makes all your dreams come true."

I said, "Thank you, Daddy—he's already off to a fantastic start."

As the doors to the sanctuary opened, I looked straight ahead to Malachi. It was as if time had stopped and all I could focus on was him. I saw him look to his brother and smile approvingly.

When I reached Malachi and my dad took his seat, Reverend Patterson recited to us what it meant to take on a spouse. He quoted from Genesis 2:23–24:

She is part of my own flesh and bone! She will be called "woman," because she was taken out of man." This explains why a man leaves his father and mother and is joined to his wife, and the two are united into one.

I turned to Malachi and saw that he'd started crying before anything had really been said. I wiped his tears away and squeezed his hand, because we'd beaten the odds. After the "I do's" were said, we kissed passionately in front of everyone who had come to celebrate this moment with us. Then Reverend Patterson introduced us as husband and wife and we jumped over the broom before we began our promenade down the aisle to the applause of everyone in the church.

Malachi and I along with our parents and the entire wedding party had to stay behind for photographs while all of the guests went to the reception center. Malachi and I were beaming from the excitement of our wedding. I was in a hurry to make it to our reception because I wanted to celebrate with everyone who had thought enough of us to come and witness this joyous occasion.

Once the pictures were taken, we exited the church, but much to my surprise, many guests had remained behind to see us. I looked out into the parking lot and thought I saw a familiar face, but when I strained my eyes to get a better look, all I heard was, "Look out—she has a gun!"

The last thing I remember before the bullet entered my chest was that I said to myself, *I didn't invite Lance to my wedding.* Then I fell to the ground with Malachi shielding me with his body. Before I fell into unconsciousness, I told him, "I love you and I'm sorry for everything." All I could think about was the life of my unborn child. I'd planned to surprise Malachi on our honeymoon by telling him I was pregnant.

CHAPTER 34

Who gets shot on her wedding day? This must be an episode out of *Jerry Springer*. Who would want to shoot me? I'd never done anything to anyone that would warrant this kind of retaliation. I could remember seeing Lance standing outside of the church before we were to leave for the wedding reception, but that's all I could remember. Surely Lance couldn't have been that upset about me marrying Malachi, after all, we'd been divorced for quite some time now. But if Lance had anything to do with my being in the hospital, I knew that Malachi would stop at nothing to hurt him. I didn't want him to do something that would put him back in prison. We were just married, and I wanted to be with my husband.

Speaking of Malachi, where was he? How come he wasn't at my bedside? Could it be that I'd been horribly disfigured and he couldn't stand the sight of me? I heard voices in my room, but I couldn't figure out what they were saying. All I could think about was Malachi, and the tears started to flow.

I heard Zondra's voice—she was arguing with my mother. Finally I could hear them clearly. Zondra was a true friend, and she was interrogating my mom like the skilled attorney she is, asking my mother: "How dare you invite Lance to Denise's wedding so that Rebecca Bennett could follow him and try and kill her?"

Rebecca did this to me? Oh my God, Malachi must be going crazy. I had to get back to him. I wanted to surprise him and tell him that I was pregnant with our first child. He would be so excited, and I couldn't wait to have his child. I just wished I'd had the chance to tell Malachi myself, I'm sure the hospital had already given him the news.

While listening to Zondra, I wondered: *how long have I been in this hospital? Where is my husband?* As if on cue, I heard Zondra say, "She's been in a coma for a month now, and her husband is frantic. He just lost his child, and we don't know if Denise is going to pull through this."

I began to cry hysterically now, and I could hear Zondra's surprised response. Then she started to rub my head and say, "She's waking up, and she's crying." I opened my eyes to see Zondra standing over me, rubbing my hair.

"What happened to my baby?"

As soon as the words escaped my lips, Zondra hugged me and said, "I'm sorry, honey—they couldn't save the baby."

At that moment Malachi walked in. He rushed over to my bedside and just started hugging and kissing me all over. He summoned the doctor, and soon several people were checking me out. My head was spinning. Everything was happening so fast, and I didn't understand what was going on, I needed someone to explain what had happened to me and why.

My mom stood next to the hospital window looking as though she'd aged ten years overnight. When Zondra and Malachi finally left the room, she said to me, "Oh, Niecey, I'm so sorry that this has happened to you. I love you and we're going to get you out of here and take you home as soon as we can."

Malachi must have overheard her, because suddenly he was in the room again. "I'm taking my wife home with me, but you are not welcome." He told my mom that it was because of her attempted manipulations that I'd been shot and almost killed, and he told her, "I'm not going to let you anywhere around her, I won't take any chances that you will cause her any more harm."

Mom looked from me to Malachi. "You have every right to be angry, Malachi, but that's still my daughter. I will respect the fact that she's your wife and you're just protecting her, but know that I brought her into this world, and I will be in Atlanta to make sure that my baby is alright." After this announcement, she gathered her purse and jacket and left. My mom was stubborn, but I still didn't understand what had happened on my wedding day. Everyone seemed to be pointing the finger at my mother as the reason for me being in this hospital bed.

Malachi and Zondra proved to be a force to be reckoned with when it came to protecting me. They wanted to get me out of the hospital and to my new home so that they could shield me from any danger that might be lurking around, but the doctors wouldn't release me until they'd had some time to observe me and make sure I was healthy enough.

I just wanted to go back to sleep and forget that I'd been shot by that psycho Rebecca Bennett on what was supposed to be the happiest day of my life. *She didn't kill me though—I'm still here. I may have lost my child, but I'm still alive, and I'm going to see that Rebecca never sees the light of day again.* I had to mourn the loss of my baby, but I was going to rejoice in the fact that I was now married and I was alive. I was anxious to get out of this hospital and get on with my life. This trouble would not stop me because I knew from James 1:2–4 that

When trouble comes your way, let it be an opportunity for joy. For when your faith is tested, your endurance has a chance to grow. So let it grow, for when your endurance is fully developed, you will be strong in character and ready for anything.

I was ready to face the world and whatever might come my way. I had a loving husband, a loyal friend, and the love of God in my heart. Today was just the beginning of a new start, and once I departed this hospital, I was going to live life to the fullest—at least that was my plan.

CHAPTER 35

I know that everything happens for a reason, but I wasn't too sure what the purpose of me getting shot on my wedding day was just yet. I wasn't questioning God's actions or timing, because he didn't make that fruitcake Rebecca Bennett shoot me, but it was his will that I didn't die from her murder attempt. Whatever His divine plan was, I knew there wasn't anything I couldn't do as long as I had faith. Now I was ready to move on and rebuild my life with my husband as the first step in getting myself together.

When the doctors finally gave the go-ahead, Malachi didn't hesitate to get me out of that hospital. I had explicit instructions to make sure I saw my family physician to follow up on my wound care. It was also recommended that I seek professional counseling, because the scars of gunshot victims can run deeper than the eyes can see. I said I would consider the suggestion, but assured everyone that I was just fine. All I wanted was to go home with my husband and finally have the honeymoon that had been stolen from me.

Malachi insisted that we would have plenty of time for that; he just wanted to make sure I was safe and secure. Even though Rebecca was now in a mental facility, Malachi wanted to take every precaution. The way he planned our trip from the hospital to the house, you would think he was a member of the Secret Service.

Our drive to the new house was somewhat uncomfortable. I was trying to reassure Malachi that I wasn't in any pain, but secretly I was nervous that danger might be lurking around the corner. I knew that Rebecca was far away, but the mere fact that she'd tried to assassinate me in public made me queasy. Malachi kept rubbing my hand and reassuring me that I didn't have anything to worry about because he was going to protect me. I admired the fact that he wanted to do so, but he couldn't cure the unsettling feeling in the pit of my stomach.

My in-laws were at the new house waiting for our arrival, and they were ready to dote on me and assist in my recovery. Zondra was at the house as well. When I made it inside, she hugged me as if she hadn't seen me in ages.

I told her to let me go before she smothered me, and she said, "Shut up and let me have this moment. You're my best friend, and I don't know what I would've done without you in my life."

I told her I wasn't going anywhere anytime soon, and we were going to grow old and gray together. I love that girl, and I knew I was blessed to have her in my life. Between her and Malachi, I don't know who the worst one was when it came to protecting those they loved. After the way they handled my mother in the hospital, I'd be afraid to go up against either one of them.

My mom meant well, but she crossed the line when she invited my ex-husband to my wedding. It was disrespectful, and it almost cost me my life. Good thing Lance had sense enough to remain seated when the minister did his speak-now-or-forever-hold-your-peace line. I'm so grateful that Lance kept his mouth shut, but it wouldn't have done him any good to say anything because I was going to say "I do" if it was the last thing I did. Wait a minute—it *was* almost the last thing.

When we got to my new home, I let everyone know I was ready to hear about what actually happened to me. Malachi was hesitant to discuss the incident, so I asked my best friend to tell me instead. Zondra replayed the entire episode for me as if she were doing an opening statement at trial. She said it all seemed to happen in slow motion, and pointed out that had my mother not been so spiteful, none of this wouldn't have taken place. My mother had taken it upon herself to invite Lance to my wedding, and Rebecca must have been stalking him because she followed him all the way from Miami to Georgia, then tried to kill me just to hurt him for not choosing to be with her. After she shot me, she fired off a few more rounds attempting to wound or kill Lance. When she missed him, she turned the gun on herself, but apparently it jammed, and she was knocked to the ground by one of the wedding guests.

During the shooting, everyone was scrambling about. Malachi had tried to shield me, but she said that there was blood everywhere and they didn't know where I'd been shot. My parents and sisters were hysterical, but when the emergency services arrived, I still had a faint pulse.

As my maid of honor, Zondra had to go to the wedding reception hall and break the news to everyone. Malcolm accompanied her, for which I was grateful; seeing me like that must have scared her half to death. While Zondra notified all of the wedding guests, my family and Malachi's parents followed the ambulance to the hospital. I was rushed into emergency surgery where it took the doctors four hours to remove the bullet that was lodged in my chest. Apparently, Rebecca had missed my heart by a few inches, and fortunately the bullet hadn't ruptured any of the main arteries. However, the doctors had told my family that I was still in critical condition due to the amount of blood I'd lost, and they wouldn't know exactly how much damage was done until I came out of the coma.

It wasn't until they started surgery that I began to hemorrhage and they realized I was pregnant. The doctors had to make a decision fast: either save just me or lose both me and the baby. Due to the trauma, the baby aborted itself, and the doctors were able to concentrate on doing everything they could to save my life.

I wanted to know exactly what happened to me, and I thought I was prepared to hear everything until Zondra spoke of my baby. Then I just lost it. Once she told me, I began to sob uncontrollably. Malachi tried to soothe me, but it was of no use. I was hurt, and I didn't think it was fair for me to have been shot on my wedding day or to have had my child ripped away from me in such a horrible manner. I wanted to be angry at someone—at my mom for the part she played in this story, at God for taking my precious child away, and at Rebecca for ruining everything that was good in my life. I'd been "the good girl" all of my life; I went to church, never harmed anyone, and been obedient to my parents, yet bad things still happened to me. What had I done to deserve this torment?

Malachi and Zondra tried to assure me that it was nothing that I did, and that God hadn't forsaken me. Maybe it was just going to take some time for me to figure out his will for this accident.

The more I sat and thought about my unborn child, the more I started to cry, until it was so much that I couldn't breathe. When I started gasping for air, everyone got nervous. All I know is that I felt as if I were suffocating. I could feel the perspiration run down my face, then the room began to spin and I fainted.

When I came to, I was in the hospital emergency room again. The doctor came in and told Malachi that I wasn't suffering from any physical injuries due to the gunshot, but that I'd apparently suffered an anxiety attack. He suggested I spend the night in the hospital for observation, but I was adamant I wasn't staying there. The treating physician spoke with Malachi, and my husband told the doctor he would guarantee I would rest comfortably at home. The doctor prescribed me some Lexapro just in case I had any more panic attacks.

Malachi didn't have to utter a word, as I could see the fear etched across his face. It was obvious on everyone's faces when I met them in the waiting area. Malachi announced to everyone that today was the last day we were going to relive the incident. He didn't want me to become overwhelmed with regret or remorse anymore. All of them nodded their heads in agreement as we gathered our belongings to return to my new home.

CHAPTER 36

The telephone never stopped ringing after I got back home. I was happy that everyone was concerned, but I didn't want to answer any questions about why Rebecca had tried to kill me. I was tired of reliving the incident, and I didn't want to run the risk of having another panic attack. My sisters and my dad called to make sure that Malachi was taking good care of me, so I let them know that he was doing a superb job. Everyone was still upset with my mother for her actions, and I can't say I blamed them, as I was displeased with her as well. I was glad to hear that everyone was doing well though.

My dad said he'd kept a vigil for me while I was in the hospital and that everyone in the church was praying for me. I let him know that I needed the prayers more than anything right now, because my strength and faith were really being tested. Pops said, "Denise, I want you to remember who you are, and whose you are. God is with you even until the end."

I said, "Well, Pops, I feel like I'm at my wit's end right about now, and I don't feel like hearing about God's grace and mercy. OK?"

"I understand, baby girl, but he's in the midst even when you think that you are alone." I told my dad I loved him and that he should tell Mom hello for me, then I hung up. I didn't have to be reminded that I was a child of God; it's just right now I thought my Heavenly Father was dishing out a little more punishment than I deserved.

My sisters wanted to come up and spend some time with me once they weren't so busy. After the wedding and watching over me in the hospital, they had to get back to their own lives. Deborah's salon demanded her undivided attention, and now that she had the new baby (my niece Diamond), it seemed as if she was always on the go. Diane was just as busy, she has been reserved as a fashion model host for some major events. Missing those engagements while I was in the hospital meant no income, so if she wanted to maintain the lifestyle to which she'd become accustomed, she had to get back to work. But when their schedules permitted, we were going to spend some quality time together. Even though they made me crazy sometimes, I felt like no one understood me like they did.

Meanwhile, I was trying to stay preoccupied as to not to cause my mind to become idle, as you know what they say about an idle mind. Now that I'd regained my strength, I was able to do some decorating around the house. Before we'd gotten married, Malachi had purchased a 3,500-square-foot home in the Buckhead section of Atlanta. It was a lavish four-bedroom brick home with three bathrooms and a three-car garage, complete with a swimming pool, exercise room, and large entertainment room. It was supposed to be his wedding gift to me, but our plans were interrupted. Now that I was at home and didn't have a job to run off to, Malachi told me to decorate the house in any way I saw fit.

With a house this large, it would take me quite some time to put my creative spin on things if I were doing everything myself. I was fortunate to have in-laws that were real estate moguls in the area, their gift to Malachi and I was an interior decorator who would assist me in making my visions for our dream home a reality. My having someone else around the house while Malachi was away at work also eased his mind a little and he didn't have to worry about me being alone. I knew he was only being protective of me as his wife, but sometimes I thought his actions were a little extreme. However, when I voiced my concerns to him, he would say, "Look, woman—I made a vow to God, and I gave you my promise that I was going to take care of you, and that's what I meant. I'm not going to risk your safety or happiness for anyone."

When he spoke like that, all I could do was listen. He still had this commanding presence about him. The way he was so authoritative towards me was kind of sexy, and I liked it. When he advised me that there were some things I must trust him on, I just uttered, "OK."

As Veronica, the interior decorator, was my babysitter for the day, I made sure that she earned her money. We visited Home Depot and Lowe's for paints and fixtures, then we stopped at Michael's and Hobby Lobby for arts and craft items. Finally we went to Pier 1 and Target for accessories for the bedrooms. I wanted each room to represent something different. I had so many ideas in my head, and Veronica knew who to contact for the labor portion of our project. All systems were go, and I as long as I stayed busy, I could forget my worries.

It took me and Veronica close to four months to complete every room just the way that I wanted them. Malachi was patient throughout the entire process, promising he wouldn't peek at any of the rooms until they were completely finished.

I had spent so much time watching home improvement shows that it had proven fairly easy to convey my vision to the interior decorator. I wanted my master bedroom to be a place of tranquility—one my husband could relax in when he came home from a hard day of work. The room did not disappoint: it was designed like a palace with colors of sage and gold. There was a television over the fireplace while the adjoining bathroom had a jet bathtub and separate shower. I knew I had done a good job because Malachi would fall asleep in his king-sized bed as soon as his head hit the pillow.

My two guest rooms were vibrant. I wanted one to look like a country inn, so Veronica suggested sea blue for the walls and white fixtures throughout the room. It was fabulous, especially since I hand selected every piece of furniture from antique stores or bargain shops. My other guest room was red and white, and I accented the room with black furniture. My husband was born and raised in Atlanta, and he was a die-hard Falcons fan. To surprise him, I decorated the entertainment room with Falcon colors and memorabilia. Zondra represented a few of the players on the team , so she had two jerseys and football helmets signed by the team and gave them to me to hang on the walls.

When I showed the room to Malachi, you would have thought he was a kid in a candy store. He jumped up and down and picked me up and hugged me. He said that he loved everything, especially the flat screen television on the wall and the movie theatre seats I had installed. I told him that this was his private sanctuary, a place where he could have his friends over and just hang out with the boys.

Our gym was equipped with the latest exercise machines: we had free weights, cardio machines, and a sauna. I had no excuse now for not working out.

I had one more room to show Malachi, and I made him cover his eyes before we entered. When I opened the door, I knew it would take Malachi's breath away, but I had no idea it would render him speechless. I'd turned the last room into a nursery because I wanted to start a family with my husband.

Malachi just looked at me and rubbed my cheek. I felt my lip quiver, but I wouldn't let any tears escape from my eyes. Malachi said "Denise, I know that losing the baby really hurt you, and what happened to you isn't easy to forget, but I think that it's time to do what the doctor recommended. You need to go talk to someone, baby."

I backed away from Malachi and got ready for what would be our first real fight. I told him, "No one will ever be able to understand how I feel, and talking to someone isn't going to change the fact that my baby was stolen from me."

"I know, but you can't keep doing this to yourself. Maybe it wasn't the right time for us to have a baby, especially since we're just starting out."

I yelled at him, "Well, what am I supposed to do all day long while you're gone and I don't have anyone to talk to or anything to do?"

"Baby, you can do anything that you want to do. How about going down to the office to see if you can give my parents a hand? I'm sure they would love to have you around. Or since you've done such a good job decorating the house, why don't you get on the computer and see if one of the local colleges is offering an interior decorating course?"

If I'd been thinking rationally, Malachi's ideas would have seemed like good ones, but something else was igniting the rage that I felt within. "You promised to make me happy, and right now the only thing that would make me happy is having a baby."

I could tell he was becoming frustrated. He said, "Denise, if I thought that would ease your pain, I would have the baby for you, but everything happens in God's perfect timing, and you very well know you can't rush him."

If my eyes were daggers, I would have sliced Malachi to shreds. I left him standing in the nursery while I went to our bedroom to cry myself to sleep.

CHAPTER 37

When I woke up the next morning, my eyes were swollen from crying so much. I could smell the breakfast that Malachi was preparing downstairs, so I headed to the shower before he returned to the room to at least make myself somewhat presentable. When I came out of the bathroom, Malachi had breakfast on a tray to serve me in bed. I looked at him and felt awful at how I'd behaved the night before.

My husband looked at me and said, "Get back in bed, Denise—I want to talk to you." I felt like a young child getting ready for a stern reprimand. Malachi said, "Denise, last night was the last night that you will go to bed angry with me for something that isn't my fault. Now, you're my wife and I love you, but things aren't getting any better with you. I've done all that I know how to do, but now I need help. That's why I spoke with the pastor of my church, and he agreed to come over and counsel us and have prayer."

I could feel my blood begin to boil, and Malachi must have been able to sense it. He said "Before you disagree, let's just hear him out. I think it will do us both some good. We can get past this, Denise, and we're going to do it together."

I knew deep down inside that he was absolutely correct, but everything in me wanted to protest this decision that he'd made without my permission. He could have his pastor come over all he wanted to, and I would even listen, but it didn't mean that I would "hear" anything he had to say. If Malachi knew me like he thought he did, he would let me work things out on my own, because the way I was feeling, I just might say something to hurt his pastor's feeling and embarrass my husband in the process. But if that's what Malachi wanted, then he would have no one else to blame but himself if things didn't work out.

That evening when Malachi arrived home from work, he showered and changed to get ready to greet our guest. I hadn't been to church that much since my move to Atlanta, and Malachi didn't push the subject, he knew I was having a spiritual battle and just needed time to find that balance once again.

When Reverend Patterson and his wife Tabitha arrived at our home, they reminded me of a fake Creflo and Taffy Dollar, who were pastors of a mega-church here in Atlanta. I was a dutiful host and I offered them beverages, but they declined. The reverend said that he was here at the request of Malachi that had arisen from the meetings they'd been having. I shot a glance at my husband, letting him know this was already getting off to a rocky start.

Reverend Patterson said, "Malachi came to me for spiritual guidance. He also wanted to make sure he was doing all that he could as your husband to assist you in your recovery from your accident."

I refused to open my mouth; instead, I just sat there like a mute. He continued, "We aren't here to tell you that you have no right to be angry. I could never understand what it's like to carry a child and then lose it in such a horrible manner."

Out of everything that happened to me, it's talking about my baby that could send me over the edge. I might not have been paying him any attention, but when he mentioned my baby, I had to tell him a thing or two. I stood up and said, "That's right—I don't expect you to understand how I feel. You could never understand just how empty I feel because I can't give my husband the one thing in the world that was created out of love and should have been a blessing from God."

Malachi came to stand next to me, saying, "Baby, don't get angry—they're just here to help us through this." I told him I wasn't going to let people who knew nothing about me tell me to get over the loss of my child.

That's when Tabitha Patterson spoke up. "No, Denise, others may not understand you, but I do." I looked at her and waited for her to continue. "My husband and I had been trying to have a baby for a very long time. We'd been to numerous fertility specialists and spent thousands of dollars on treatments guaranteeing us we would become parents. But nothing seemed to work.

"We were prepared to just enjoy our lives without children when I learned in my second month that I was finally pregnant. We did everything that expecting parents should have done when preparing for the birth of a child. I watched the things I ate, I made sure I asked all the right questions during my doctor visits, and I was real careful with the miracle that I was carrying. I could feel this new life forming within me, and I was prepared to share my testimony with everyone about waiting on the Lord.

"Then in the beginning of my fourth month of pregnancy, I got violently ill and the doctor put me on bed rest. I stayed put, but then one night at 2:46 a.m., I woke up and felt the warm liquid soaking my bed. I screamed to Kendrick that something was wrong. I knew before I ever made it to the hospital that I had lost my baby, and I was angry at the world."

When Tabitha spoke, I felt as if I had found a kindred spirit. I asked her, "What happened?"

"I just miscarried. There was no particular reason as to why I lost the baby, and I couldn't understand how a God I'd faithfully served would allow me to go through all of the emotions and preparations for this child just to take it away from me. I felt I couldn't talk to my husband, and I shut everyone out, just like you're doing."

I asked her how she got through it. She said, "With the help of my husband and much prayer. I never gave up hope that God would enrich our lives with children. That's why I'm here today, Denise—we have three boys now, but I wouldn't have a testimony if I hadn't passed that test. God doesn't make any mistakes, sweetheart. I'm not telling you what I've heard—I'm talking about what I know."

After I finally heard everything Tabitha said, I just sobbed, even though I was still so angry and felt like I'd been robbed of my joy. Malachi hugged me and began to cry also. I'd been so consumed with my own thoughts that I didn't think of how he must have felt to lose his child. I was happy that Malachi thought enough of our relationship to seek the counsel of godly people. I'm the one that likes to hold everything in, because I don't want to burden others with my problems but having this couple confess their loss, let me know that by sharing I just might be able to help someone else who is going through a tough trial.

The reverend said that he wanted to end the evening in prayer, so we all bowed our heads and he quoted from Proverbs 3:4–6:

Father God, we humbly come to you and ask that you bless this young couple as they mend their hearts and minds over the loss of their child. Lord we know that you are too just to do any wrong and too wise to make a mistake. I ask now that you unite them and remind them that they can overcome any ordeal as long as they trust in the Lord with all their heart, lean not on their own understanding, in all their ways acknowledge you and you will direct their path.

I thanked him and his wife for coming out and sharing their story with us. I did feel much better knowing that it was alright to be sad, but God had not brought me this far to leave me. Malachi had been a tremendous support, and it was time I devoted a little more time and attention to him. He worked hard to support us, and I didn't experience this thing alone, he was there every step of the way. We'd come so far that it just didn't make sense to go backwards. Tonight I let go of the past and put everything in God's hand.

After saying good-bye to the Pattersons, I escorted my husband upstairs and made love to him, and I could feel all of his tension escape from within.

CHAPTER 38

Good thing I had that session with the Pattersons, it helped to prepare me for what was coming next. It had been close to seven moths since my wedding when the investigator on the case contacted Malachi and me to let us know that Rebecca had been ruled fit to stand trial, so a hearing had been scheduled for her to enter her plea. Now the God in me felt sorry for her, and I asked that she be forgiven for her act of vengeance against me. But the unGodly side of me wanted her to cook in the electric chair for everything that she'd done to me both past and present.

Malachi asked the investigator if it was necessary for us to be in the courtroom, and he said that it would improve the chance that she wouldn't be released on bail before the start of the trial. Malachi squeezed my hand and told the detective we would be there.

The court proceedings were to be held in Savannah; that's where the women's prison was located, and where Rebecca was now being housed after having been transferred from the mental institution to the psychiatric ward of the jail. For moral support, my entire family showed up for the proceedings. My parents and sisters, my in-laws, and Zondra: everyone wanted to get a good look at the fruit loop who had tried to kill me.

The only one in the courtroom for Rebecca was her mother, or at least I assumed it was her since Rebecca's attorney kept turning around to console her. I almost didn't recognize Rebecca, she didn't look anything like her normal self. Apparently they had her medicated (heavily I might add); her hair was disheveled, and she was damn near drooling all over the table. I don't know what kind of drugs she was on, but she was definitely in La-La Land.

I didn't know why that investigator had us drive all the way down here, shoot we were in court less than thirty minutes. The only thing the judge asked was, "How does your client plead, counselor," and Rebecca's lawyer responded by saying, "Not guilty by reason of temporary insanity, your honor." At that announcement, Rebecca's mother let out a loud yelp, but Rebecca just sat at the attorney's table rocking back and forth as if she were oblivious to everything around her. I hoped they'd make her lucid enough to stand trial, at least long enough to explain why she hated me enough to see me dead.

When Rebecca's mother got up to leave the courtroom, she stood in front of my parents, pointed at Pops, and said, "This is your fault—you will pay for what you did to my daughter."

My dad looked at her and said, "I already have." Then she stormed out of the courthouse. My mom was infuriated and started going on about how craziness must run in their family, because the apple didn't fall far from the tree. I don't know if those two were playing crazy or not, but I needed to know when the trial would be set to start. The leading prosecutor for the state indicated that he was still building his evidence against Rebecca, and he would have to interview us for his case, but that his office would contact us to schedule an appropriate time for him to take our depositions in Atlanta.

Having Zondra there really made a difference, as she was able to explain all of the legal terminology. I learned that there would probably be another hearing in the next few weeks to set a trial date. Rebecca had a public defender, her defense probably wouldn't get any better than temporary insanity, and that would work only if her attorney could get her to communicate. "Yeah, good luck with that one," I told Zondra.

Rebecca looked nothing now like the girl with whom we'd gone to college with. That woman today looked so spaced out that I don't think she knew what planet she was on. But then again, this was Rebecca Bennett I was referring to, and she could be playing the role of a lifetime. If she was acting, she could give Halle Berry a run for her money next time for the Best Actress Oscar.

The entire family was gathered, and we hadn't seen each other in a while; everyone wanted to remain in Savannah for a little longer. We decided to eat lunch at Fatz Café, a restaurant that serves southern specialties. Everyone was in agreement for staying the night in Savannah, we all rented rooms at a local hotel and decided that we would enjoy each other's company and depart the next day.

Having my sisters and Zondra with me put me at ease about the entire ordeal, and it was good just to laugh again. As we sat at the table in the restaurant with everyone feeling like old times, Diane started asking inappropriate questions. She opened her big mouth and began, "Malcolm, you know Zondra is a part of our family, and since you all have been dating for what seems like forever, what exactly are your intentions?"

Zondra looked at Diane and then to me, whispering, "Your sister is so uncouth."

I looked at Diane, but all she did was shrug her shoulders and say, "What?"

Malcolm looked uneasy as he told Diane, "Maybe you should worry about your own man, and why you are here A-L-O-N-E." That got everyone to laugh, and it broke the tension that was so obvious to me.

Mom and Pops were more quiet than usual, and I tried to engage them in conversation along with Malachi's folks. But my parents said they were really tired and it had been a long day, so after lunch they were going back to the hotel to rest.

After we finished eating, we went shopping at the local mall. It wasn't much of a mall, and I guessed that's why Savannah was better known for its history. By the time we made it back to the hotel, we were all exhausted from the day's events. Malachi and Malcolm decided to go to the Sports Bar to watch television while their parents relaxed in their room. Me and the girls gathered in my sisters' room so that Deb could do my hair which she said looked a hot mess. I told her, "I've been busy with so many other things that hair was the last thing on my agenda."

She said, "Girl, you ain't been married to Malachi that long—I suggest you continue to do everything that allowed you to snag him."

"For your information, Malachi will tell you that my hair wasn't one of the things that attracted him to me. He liked me instead for the way I walked, talked, and smiled."

Deborah laughed at me. "Girl, please—that man was incarcerated. A three-hundred-pound bearded woman would look good to him under those circumstances. Not saying that you look that bad, but your hair is in desperate need of attention."

"Well, shut up then and do what you do best."

Diane always had something smart to say, so she chimed in "Ya'll both are pitiful. It's obvious I was the one blessed with beauty, body, and brains. I'm the complete package." Zondra, Deb, and I just burst out laughing. That girl still thinks the world revolves around her.

After Deb washed, conditioned, and dried my hair, she was able to trim the edges and give me a nice, bouncy Doobie wrap. She commented, "Now my brother-in-law will remember why he fell in love with you." That girl was a miracle worker on people's heads because I hardly resembled the old me.

By this time, Diane had fallen asleep, and Zondra and I left to go be with our men, who we knew had probably returned to the room already. I kissed my sisters good night and agreed to meet them for brunch in the hotel lobby in the morning.

Zondra told me later that when she went to her room, she was still secretly bothered by Diane's question to Malcolm during lunch. Never one to hold her tongue, when she got ready for bed, Zondra asked Malcolm, "Where are we going?"

Malcolm replied, "We're going home to Atlanta tomorrow."

Zondra then said, "No, where is this relationship going? I mean, just a few months ago, you were standing up at your brother's wedding rehearsal dinner telling everyone just how much you loved me, yet when Diane put you on the spot this afternoon, you didn't have anything to say. Why is that?"

Malcolm told her, "Look, Z, you're not in a courtroom, and you're not cross-examining me. There's nothing wrong with me. I love you woman—don't let that lonely Diane put no mess in your head, alright?"

However, the lawyer in Zondra wouldn't let Malcolm have the last word: "I'm not letting anyone put anything in my head. She just asked a question, and I'd like to know the answer."

Malcolm came and stood in front of Zondra. "I said that we were fine, Z—now drop the subject." Zondra wasn't used to any man telling her what to do, but she said she left Malcolm alone after that and went to bed wondering when he was going to break her heart.

Even though she didn't tell me the story until later, after knowing Zondra for so long, I could tell that something was wrong with her the next morning when we all sat down for brunch, Malcolm wasn't himself either, and they both looked like they hadn't slept too well.

At the table, Deb looked at me and asked, "What happened to your hair after I spent all that time fixing it?"

"What do you think happened to it? I'm still in the honeymoon phase of my marriage."

She looked at me and Malachi and said, "I need to get back to my own husband and kids and get away from all of you freaks." We just laughed and told her to stop hating on the love.

Everyone enjoyed brunch before we had to get back on the road. My sisters had a long drive ahead of them; they were driving back to Miami with my parents. Mr. and Mrs. Donahue were going to stay in Savannah for a few more days just to relax, while Zondra, Malcolm, Malachi, and I were driving back to Atlanta together. We all hugged and said our good-byes before we checked out of the hotel. Now all we had to do was wait until the *State of Georgia vs. Rebecca Bennett* came to trial.

Once Zondra, Malcolm, my husband, and I were in the truck headed back home, I asked them, "What is the problem with you two? I could feel the tension between the both of you while we were eating." Malachi just looked at me in the rearview mirror. I stared back at him and said, "What? We're family and if they have a problem, we all have a problem. Now what's the damn problem?"

Zondra asked, "Yeah, Malcolm—what's the damn problem?" Those twin brothers were exactly alike. I could see Malcolm's face becoming tense, then Malachi looked at him and just shook his head as if to tell him not to respond.

Malachi then looked at me from the rearview mirror again and said, "Mind your own business, Denise. Let my brother handle his own business. He and Zondra are adults, and they are capable of fixing whatever problems you think they may have."

I told him, "I wouldn't be a true friend if I didn't voice my concerns."

Out of the blue, Malcolm quoted 1 Thessalonians 4:11: "This should be your ambition, to live a quiet life, minding your own business"

"Look who's been paying attention in Bible study" I said as I nudged the back of his head from the backseat. Everyone started laughing and we drove the rest of the way home without me interfering in their business. Besides, Zondra would tell me everything when she got the chance to interrogate Malcolm again.

CHAPTER 39

It was a few weeks after we returned from Savannah that I received a telephone call from Malcolm. When I asked him what was up, he told me he wanted to talk to me about Zondra and could I meet him for lunch so that he could explain further? Malcolm's call made me nervous, but I didn't want to think the worst about our impromptu meeting to discuss my friend. We decided to meet at P. F. Chang's Chinese restaurant.

When I arrived, he was already seated, and he motioned for me to join him. I sat down and gave the waiter my lunch selection. Malcolm said, "Look, I know that you all think I've been acting weird when it comes to my relationship with Zondra, but I love that woman and she knows it. I've just wanted to do something for quite some time now, and I didn't know exactly how I should go about it. Since you're her best friend and my sister-in-law, I came to you for your advice."

I said, "Sure, Malcolm—what's on your mind?"

He said, "Well, it's like this, Zondra is a very independent woman and she's used to doing things on her own terms. She's very headstrong, she's smart and classy, but then she can be that ride-or-die chick every man wants."

I laughed because he had Zondra down pat. "I know all of that, Malcolm, and …"

"I just don't know what she would think about this." He pulled a black box out of his pocket and slid it across the table in my direction. My mouth fell open and I started to fan myself with my hands because I was so excited for my friend. I opened it and all I could say was "Damn!" It had to be most gorgeous 3.5 carat princess cut engagement ring I'd ever seen.

"What do you think she'll say?"

"Boy, you better quit playing and do the damn thing. Why do you think she's been uptight for the past few weeks?"

He said "Huh?"

"Malcolm, get a clue—Zondra has been feeling like you were losing interest in her. She thought that's why you didn't answer my sister Diane's question when we were in Savannah."

He laughed. "Then I'd better plan to pop the question real soon, but first I must swear you to secrecy."

I held up my hand. "Boy Scout's honor."

"You weren't a Boy Scout."

We finished lunch, and Malcolm kissed me good-bye before we went our separate ways in the parking lot. I couldn't wait to get home and share the news with Malachi.

I should've known Malcolm would confer with his twin brother before asking me anything. As soon as he got home that night, Malachi asked, "How did things go at lunch?"

I said, "I was sworn to secrecy, and if you know we had lunch, then you probably know that things went well."

"Yeah—I just wanted to hear your version. Do you think Z will like the ring?"

"Like it? She'll be doing cartwheels."

"That's what I told Malcolm."

My man looked as if he were exhausted. I asked him, "Do you want something special for dinner?"

Malachi arched his eyebrow and said, "Forget the dinner—why don't we just have dessert for starters, then we can go out later for the real meal."

"That's a great idea," I told him as I led him upstairs and showed him that dessert didn't always have to follow the main course.

My session with Malachi really worked up my appetite. I decided we would have dinner at my favorite restaurant, The Cheesecake Factory, and I invited Malcolm and Zondra to dine with us. We talked and laughed all through dinner.

After we made our cheesecake selections, Malcolm excused himself to go to the restroom. Our dessert arrived at the table via Malcolm carrying the tray, and he presented Zondra with hers first. "Malcolm, what on earth are you doing?" she asked.

"Something I should've done a long time ago." Malachi and I just sat there as privileged witnesses for what was about to unfold.

Zondra took the black box from the plate, and Malcolm grabbed her hands to stand up. He said, "I don't want you to second guess how I feel about you any more. I've confessed to my love for you in front of family, and now I'm doing it again in a room full of strangers." Malcolm got down on one knee. "Z, I love you more today than I did yesterday. Every day that we're together, my love for you grows stronger. I don't ever want to lose that feeling and I don't want to lose you. Will you please marry me?"

Zondra said, "Of course I will." Malcolm slipped the ring on her finger, and they kissed in front of everyone to seal the deal. The entire restaurant erupted in applause.

Malachi and I congratulated them, and I said to Zondra, "Hello, Mrs. Donahue."

"Same to you, Mrs. Donahue," she said back. We laughed because now my best friend was going to be my sister. This was a dinner to remember: my best friend was engaged, and our family was expanding. Malcolm couldn't stop smiling, and if I knew Zondra, she would keep a smile on his face for the rest of their lives.

CHAPTER 40

Now it was my turn to devote my time to helping Zondra plan her wedding because she was a nervous wreck. She really didn't want anything elaborate, yet Malcolm insisted on something formal. I was so consumed with things for Zondra that I almost forgot I was approaching my first wedding anniversary. Malachi wanted to make sure that I didn't dwell on the tragedy of the day so he wanted to take me someplace exotic to celebrate. I told him that I didn't have a job to report to and I was game for whatever. I wanted to surprise him with a nice gift for our anniversary and I was unsure what would be the perfect gift. When I told Zondra about our anniversary plans, I could see the wheels in her brain start moving. She said, "Girl, that's it. I'll ask Malcolm if we could get married on the beach in Jamaica."

"Sounds good to me," I replied.

That was our agenda: setting a date for a beach wedding in Jamaica. Zondra said that she didn't want anyone there except for the immediate family. That was arranged as well. I took care of all the preparations so all we had to do was pack our bags. The wedding was less than three months away and Zondra kept busy by trying to clear her caseload; she didn't want to have to be summoned home because a client had an emergency. The other attorneys in her office understood her commitment to her clients and agreed to assist her. They also wished her well on her engagement and the women in the office even threw her a bridal shower before we were scheduled to depart for the Caribbean.

The four of us flew down to Jamaica together with our families due to arrive later that same evening. Zondra's aunts were coming along with her little brother and sister and Malcolm's parents. The wedding was going to be very small and intimate, but that's how Zondra wanted it. I've never seen my friend happier than she was at this moment. Although she tried to appear in control, I could tell she was nervous. She even admitted to me that she had bubble guts and couldn't fight the urge to run to the bathroom. I told her that it was just her nerves and she better get it all out before the ceremony because the only place she could run after that was straight into the ocean.

When everyone arrived, we met for dinner at a place outside the resort. There were a lot of introductions because many of Zondra's family hadn't met her soon-to-be in-laws. We were all happy that this day had finally arrived for her, and I couldn't think of a person (except for me) who was more deserving of a man as considerate, dedicated, and loyal as Malcolm (other than his identical twin brother who had the same qualities).

It was my turn to give the toast for the evening, so I stood up and requested everyone's attention. I said, "I would like to give a toast to my best friend who I've known since we were college roommates. She is definitely a rare breed, and Malcolm is indeed the lucky one who is getting this treasure. I would like to credit myself with introducing the two of you, which ultimately got us to this point, but the search was over when you first met. The both of you compliment one another so well that you were definitely meant for each other. So here's to lasting love and to growing old together." Everyone saluted the bride and groom and clapped for them.

Then it was Malachi's turn to say a few words to his brother. He turned to look at Zondra and Malcolm, then said, "For over thirty years, Malcolm, you have been my better half, and there hasn't been anything that we haven't been through together. You are my brother and my best friend. Now I gladly pass the reins over to Zondra to take my place. I welcome her into our family with open arms. She joins my wife as the daughters Mom never had. Here's to a long, prosperous, and amazing life together."

When I looked at my in-laws, Mrs. Donahue was wiping the tears away from her eyes. I winked at her to let her know I loved her.

After a long night of eating and drinking, we were exhausted and thought it best to turn in and save some of our energy for the next day. In keeping with tradition, I made Malachi spend the night in the room with his brother while Zondra and I shared a room. Malachi said, "OK, honey—that's fair. Besides I have to get my surprise ready for you."

I told my husband that now wasn't the time for fun and games because we were here on serious business. Once we got Malcolm and Zondra married, then we could enjoy our anniversary. He assured me his surprise wouldn't interfere with the wedding, but he just needed to make sure everything was in place. I said, "Alright, Mr. Donahue, but I have my eye on you."

Zondra and I talked well into the early morning. She was elated at getting married, but she was nervous about having to balance a husband and a demanding career. I had to persuade her to stop worrying. I insisted that the Donahue men were more than capable of taking care of their women— I was living proof of that. "Besides," I said. "Malcolm isn't threatened by your success. He applauds all of your ideas and efforts, and he supports any decisions that you make."

Zondra agreed with my assessment. I told her to look at Malachi, these men were cut from the same cloth, and if nothing else they could be trusted to do what was right when it came to the people they loved. They embodied the three most important things a man should have when taking on a wife. First, they didn't have a problem professing their love for their women. Second, they could certainly provide for their families, and third, they were willing to die trying to protect those they loved.

I finished up by saying, "Girl, you are worrying too much when everything is as it should be."

"Yeah, you're right girl," Zondra admitted. "I'm just tripping. I love that man with every fiber of my being—I just don't want to disappoint him in any way."

"Just keep being his freak of the week and he can't be disappointed." We went to sleep laughing that night with our hearts and mind at ease because we knew what it was to find your soul mate.

CHAPTER 41

The day that we'd all been waiting for had finally arrived. I got Zondra ready and waiting downstairs. The men and other guests were already on the beach standing by. The event organizer gave us our cue to walk down the pathway to where the wedding would be taking place. Everything was perfect; even the weather was just right, and the sun wasn't blazing hot.

Everyone was dressed in white linen, which was nice and elegant. I strode down the beach with Zondra following me. As I went up to stand next to Malachi, I noticed our guests had grown to include my parents as well as my sisters and their families. Malachi, looked at me and said, "Surprise—today is your wedding day also." I was stunned. This man could still knock the wind out of me.

Zondra took her place next to Malcolm and said, "Gotcha!" I couldn't believe it: everyone was in on the surprise except for me. Malachi had managed to put together a recommitment ceremony, including bringing in all of my family without one of my big- mouth sisters spilling the beans. This was definitely the ultimate wedding anniversary gift and I could never top his surprise.

The minister officiating the occasion smiled as we all got settled in our places. Zondra and Malcolm exchanged their vows first, then it was Malachi's and my turn. We were all pronounced and presented as husband and wife, I don't know about Zondra, but I was walking on cloud nine. The entire family celebrated at a feast fit for a king and his royal court. My wedding was better the second time around. I couldn't wait until it was over to show my husband his gift.

My husband and I and my new sister-in-law and her husband left our guests to continue dancing and dining until their hearts were content while we escaped upstairs to have our own private celebration. Malachi asked, "Honey, were you surprised?"

I replied, "You did a superb job, Mr. Donahue—now let me show you what I have in store for you." I undressed my man and led him to the bathroom where we took a shower together and did some freaky things to one another. Malachi lathered my body and caressed my breasts. He stayed hard for me as I teased him with my sensual touches.

When I turned around for him to rinse off my breasts, he stopped and asked, "What's that?"

I said, "What, this little thing? It's just a tattoo to cover my bullet wound, and it's my surprise to you." He looked closer to read the inscription on my chest: "My heart belongs to Malachi," and it had a drawing of two joined hearts.

My husband beamed with joy and said, "That's right, woman—you belong to me and I belong to you. I love you, Denise, and I want to know if you are really you happy."

"Of course. You said that you would make me the happiest woman in the world, and you haven't disappointed me." He picked me up and carried me to the bed soaking wet. We made a mess of the bed that night, but that man had me yearning for more. I never thought that I could climax as many times as I did that night before he sent me to bed exhausted.

But by the morning I was re-energized and ready for another round. Malachi said, "Dang, girl—you wore me out last night, and you're ready for more?"

I told him, "That's right—I'm going to drain you of all your natural juices."

He laughed and said, "We're going to have to take you and your comedy act on the road." I expressed to him that he was the only one laughing, and he was going to have to surrender to my wishes right now because I wanted to make him say my name.

When we finally did come out of the room to join our families, it was midday. We wanted to enjoy some of the sights the island offered in its tour packages. The older folks wanted to stay near the hotel and walk along the beach, which was fine with us. Everyone else had just come down for the wedding and were only staying the weekend, whereas Zondra, Malcolm, Malachi, and I were going to be here for an entire week. I didn't have a honeymoon the first time Malachi and I got married, but it didn't even matter now. God timed everything perfectly and as usual, he was right on time.

Our week in Jamaica flew by. We went to the alligator farm, took a water rafting trip, rode horses in the mountains, and went shopping in the market area. Malachi and I made love in the water, on the beach by moonlight, in the elevator, and any other place we thought was sufficiently secluded. When Zondra and I spoke, I told her about some of our sexcapades, and she said, "I should be taking some tips from you—looks like I'm not the only freak in this family. These Donahue men don't know who they're messing with huh." I gave her a high five and we laughed together.

None of us were ready to go back home, but we couldn't stay on the island forever. Besides, Zondra had been away from her practice long enough. I told her that before she went into the office, she needed to run to a hair dresser because her do was done. She said, "Girl, I know. Between getting in the water every day and Malcolm playing with it at night, I look like a pure mess right about now. I just hope I don't scare the man off."

"Now you know he ain't hardly going nowhere, so you can just get that thought right out of your mind."

While flying back home, we were all seated in the same row on the airplane, and our husbands (it was funny saying that now) were going back and forth telling us stories about the pranks they'd use to pull when they were kids, including some of the things for which they'd never gotten caught for. Zondra said, "Honey, as your attorney, I'm advising you against incriminating yourself."

Malcolm replied, "Baby, it's alright—as my wife, you can't be called to testify against me. Besides, my dear old brother will do my time for me if I ask him to."

I chimed in and said, "No, brother won't—we've traveled down that road before and we're not interested in going back down it again. What your brother can do for you is keep some money on your books so you have enough to do your little shopping in the commissary." We laughed so loudly the flight attendant had to come by and advise us to keep our chatter down. We apologized for disturbing anyone, but we kept telling jokes.

I could get used to times like these, and it seemed as if we were going to be seeing a lot of each other. Shoot, Malachi and Malcolm couldn't get enough of each other. You would think that being trapped in the womb with someone for nine months, then having to live a life with someone who looks just like you, would be tiresome and that they would be looking to create their own identities, but nope, not those two. Even though they saw each other at work, they still talked on the phone about four times a day, and I could swear they had some kind of weird mental telepathy going on where they could read each other's minds or something. When we would all go out and meet up, more than once they'd arrived wearing the exact same clothes even though they didn't coordinate it.

Now that Malcolm and Zondra would be living only a few miles away from us, we were sure to be entertaining at each other's houses on a regular basis. Once she got married, Zondra didn't sell her home; she decided to turn it into a bed-and-breakfast inn. It was a great idea; her home was located in an upscale area that also was in the vicinity of some of Atlanta's most interesting tourist attractions. For those just passing through town, Zondra's home was the perfect place to lay their heads for the night. She hired staff to run the place while she was busy working and settling into her new home with Malcolm.

She told me that was one of the business ventures which she was interested in after she finished her legal career, but she didn't know if she could juggle everything, especially since during their honeymoon, Malcolm had kept talking about starting a family. I told her the same thing that Tabitha Patterson told me when she came to our house to pray for me: "Listen, Z, don't worry about the things that you don't have control over. Just live and let things come as they may. The children will come; the job may change, but just live in the moment."

She looked at me and said, "That's exactly what I'm going to do."

CHAPTER 42

I was on such a high after we came back from Jamaica that the only thing that could burst my bubble was news about Rebecca Bennett. Apparently while we were in Jamaica, the prosecutor's office had been trying to reach us to schedule our interviews for the upcoming trial. I guess the sooner I got it over with, the better it would be for me and my family. No one wanted to keep reliving that incident, but it had to be done in order to put Rebecca behind bars.

The attorney was coming in over the weekend, which was perfect; Malachi wasn't working and would be available for moral support. Zondra was going to be present as well to make sure that the questions didn't offend me or were irrelevant. Plus they would have their own stories to tell as witnesses.

I spoke with Tabitha Patterson to let her know that I needed some special prayers in order to talk about my ordeal. After their visit to our home, the Pattersons had become more than just our pastor and first lady—they were also mentors and friends. I sought their advice whenever I needed to be spiritually lifted. Right now I needed something that would get me through this tribulation. The power of prayer was tremendous and had a way of calming my nerves. I didn't want to start taking Lexapro again for my panic attacks because I didn't want to give any more recognition to Rebecca Bennett than I had to. My becoming dependent on medication to control my frame of mind would be surrendering to my fears, and I wouldn't give in to them.

I had been doing so well for so long, but in the pit of my stomach, I could tell that trouble was on the horizon. I didn't want to alarm Malachi because things between us were on track, but I just didn't know what to do; I could only mask my emotions for so long before they started to consume me and make me do something drastic.

Tabitha Patterson agreed to stop by the house on Friday evening and speak with me before I was scheduled to conduct my interview with the attorney in the prosecutor's office. Malachi could sense that I was anxious about the coming weekend, but he allowed me to work through it on my own, which I was grateful for. I didn't want him to think I was this fragile creature who got frazzled by any and everything. He stayed in his entertainment room while I spoke to Tabitha.

Tabitha sat with me in our living room, which she commented on as being a peaceful area she enjoyed every time she visited our home. I told her that the interior designer and I had put a lot of effort into making this house embody a calming, peaceful aura for us and anyone who visited. She said, "Yes, you all put the material things in here but I can tell that the spirit of the Lord also dwells in these walls."

I told her "Thank you. I give all the credit to my husband for being spiritually grounded. As the leader of this household, he has cultivated a relationship with God, and we have been blessed because of it. He has integrity, he works hard to provide for his family, he's humble, and he isn't ashamed to tell anyone that Jesus is his Lord and Savior. Because of that, in his heart is the reflection of love. Therefore, I know the presence of God is in my home, and as long as my husband is seeking the Lord in all that he does, then I will follow him and know that our home will be blessed."

Tabitha said, "You've said a mouthful. I should invite you to give that same speech to our couples' ministry."

I said, "No, really, I was married once before, and I know now that it wasn't built on a spiritual platform, and we weren't equally yoked. I can tell the difference now. Malachi knows what his role and responsibilities are as a husband, and he always considers how his actions will affect our lives. Then he always does what's best for our household. I didn't have that before. My ex-husband would jump when his mother or job called—he wasn't guided by the Lord. I'm not saying that he was a bad guy, but he just wasn't the right man for me."

Tabitha listened attentively. "Denise, you're absolutely correct. When God designs something for us, he's doesn't do it halfway. Sometimes we may not understand why things occur the way they do, but in the end we're stronger because of it, and it brings us to where God wants us to be. When we as people feel as if we are experiencing so many difficulties in our life, we have to understand that God is our Heavenly Father, and what we've deemed as difficulties are just the way he accomplishes his goals. He's developing our character so he also has to discipline us at times. Things don't happen because we're bad and God wants us to suffer—he wants us to trust and believe that he has our back no matter what we go through."

I told Tabitha that I really appreciated her friendship. After moving here from South Carolina, other than my best friend, I didn't know anyone except for my husband and his family, but Tabitha had become a confidant. Her purpose in life was definitely being a friend. We hugged and I told her, "I kind of got off of the real reason I called you over here, but now that you're here, I feel so much better."

Tabitha said, "Well, then my mission is accomplished so I'll be going, but before I leave I want to have a word of prayer with you and Malachi."

I summoned Malachi from his television room and he came up to join us. We held hands and Tabitha said, "Lord, we come to you this evening with open hearts and open minds. We ask for strength during this time of battle, and we're trusting and believing that we will be victorious because we're walking by faith and not by sight. Lord, remove this fear from Denise and remind her of your word when you said in Isaiah chapter eight, verses thirteen and fourteen, 'Do not fear anything except the Lord Almighty. He alone is the Holy One. If you fear him, you need fear nothing else. He will keep you safe.' In closing, we thank you for all of your blessings. We love you, honor, and adore you. In Jesus name we pray, amen."

When we were done, Malachi and I walked Tabitha to the door and said our good-byes. After she was gone, he looked at me and asked, "Honey, are you alright?" I smiled at my husband lovingly and answered him by kissing him and leading him back into our living room area where we made love in the same room we'd received the prayers and blessings from Tabitha Patterson. As she'd attested to the Lord being present in this house, I hope he had his eyes shut during our romp on the living room floor because it definitely wasn't something I wanted the Lord to witness.

CHAPTER 43

My husband and I were anxiously waiting along with Zondra for the prosecuting attorney. Mr. Davenport arrived at our home at 10 a.m. He'd said that my interview wouldn't take that long. In fact, he had already gotten enough from the statements of other witnesses and the physical evidence to prove beyond a reasonable doubt that Rebecca had been the one to shoot me. He just wanted to let me know what was going to be presented to the court, but he doubted it would be necessary for me to take the witness stand.

I told him, "I wouldn't mind facing Rebecca. I want to look her in the eyes and let her know that she didn't win, that she didn't kill me, and that I'm happy even though she tried to destroy me." Mr. Davenport warned Malachi and me that the trial could be lengthy because they had to bring in an expert witness to determine Rebecca's mental state at the time of the shooting. He also wanted us to make sure we were prepared to listen to outlandish remarks from her defense attorney.

I let Mr. Davenport know that with everything I'd been through at the hands of Rebecca Bennett, nothing would give me greater pleasure than to witness someone trying to justify her actions or what she tried to do to me in front of all of my wedding guests, her defense would be comical. He said, "That's my opinion as well, so we offered her a plea, but they rejected it and decided to take their chances with a jury trial."

I told him, "I've known that woman for some time, and she's never been one to think logically. I'm prepared to get this over with, Mr. Davenport. I've suffered, my husband has suffered, and my entire family has suffered. It's time to put an end to this book and write something else with a happy ending."

He promised me, "You'll be able to write that book before you know it, Mrs. Donahue. I promise you I will do my job, and one way or another, Rebecca Bennett will never be allowed to rejoin society again." With his declaration, I shook his hand and began looking forward to us having our day in court.

CHAPTER 44

Rebecca's trial had been scheduled for two months after our meeting with Mr. Davenport. It was fast, but I was ready. My entire family convened once again in Savannah. The courtroom was packed. I hadn't thought this case would garner that much attention, but this was Savannah, not Atlanta, and this was an exciting, newsworthy moment for the local media.

We were all seated behind the prosecutor's table. Again the only one there in support of Rebecca was her mother. That woman looked pitiful, but she had to stand by her child. I felt sorry for her now as she'd been left to care for Rebecca's children, I thought it must be hard for her to look at them every day and not be able to explain to them why their mother did the things she did.

Before the judge entered the courtroom, the bailiff ushered Rebecca in. She didn't even look in my direction. At least her appearance was better than the first time we were in court, so they must have lowered the dosage of her psych medication and made her presentable for the trial. I couldn't wait to get my chance to tell her what I thought about her, but it would be a while before I got a chance to take the stand. Both sides had to present their opening statements.

I could tell the defense attorney wasn't prepared for this case. I'd seen enough *Court TV*, *LA Law*, and *Law & Order* as well as read enough crime stories to know that her ship was sinking fast and Rebecca would be drowning by the time the prosecutor finished his case.

Mr. Davenport's opening statement was well rehearsed, straightforward, and to the point. He began, "Ladies and gentleman of the jury, I will present to you a case that reeks of jealousy and hatred. The defendant, Rebecca Bennett, vindictively and callously sought out Mrs. Denise Donahue with the intention of killing her in cold blood on the one day every young girl dreams and plans about—her wedding day. This was supposed to be the most exciting and memorable day of her life, a day Denise was sharing with her family and friends. But that woman sitting at the defense table has held a grudge against Denise that stems all way back to their days in college. This was going to be her last chance to humiliate and destroy Denise in front of everyone, then kill herself.

"But things did not go as she had planned. She did shoot Denise, but Denise didn't die, and fortunately she is here and can testify before you about the ways Rebecca Bennett repeatedly tried to ruin her life. The defense will try to paint a picture of a woman who was raised by a single mother, who had a hard life, then became a teenaged mother and a statistic, and because of the pressures of her life, she just went insane. Well, I ask you—who in this room doesn't have daily pressures? That doesn't mean we have the right to plot, plan, and seek people out to kill them. Besides, the evidence will show Rebecca Bennett was not insane when she shot Denise Donahue. I will prove to you that she is someone who needs to be put away because she is a threat to society, and the only place she is fit to dwell is behind bars. Thank you for your attention."

Wow, I was blown away by Mr. Davenport's introduction, hearing him say all of those things about what happened made a tear come to my eyes. Malachi rubbed my shoulders in support and from her seat behind me; I could feel Zondra rub my back. I turned around to let her know that I was alright, and I saw sitting in the courtroom both my ex-boyfriend Carl Lemon and my ex-husband Lance Weldon. This was going to be interesting; all the men I'd ever loved were in the same room, with two of them having slept with Rebecca.

Zondra could see the expression on my face change when I turned around, and she was never one to be inconspicuous, she turned around as well. When she saw what I'd been looking at, she muttered, "Um, um, um! Let the games begin." If I was a smoker, I would have been outside right then huffing on some cancer sticks. If the trial was starting out with these kinds of surprises, fireworks would be sure to follow.

The defense attorney must have been taken aback or disorganized because when he got up to give his opening statement, he had to read from what was written on a legal pad instead of having it memorized. Zondra whispered to me, "We can see who studied for their exams last night."

He started off, "Good morning, ladies and gentlemen of the jury. The prosecutor would have you believe that Rebecca Bennett is a cold and calculating individual who was full of envy over Mrs. Donahue, when in fact that isn't the case at all. Here is a woman who struggled every day of her life, wanting nothing but the approval of those who loved her. She isn't mean or hateful—she just got rejected one time too many, and it pushed her over the edge from sanity to insanity. She had been rejected and denied all of her life, and she was at her breaking point and could not take the pressure anymore. At that moment in time, my client lost the ability to distinguish fantasy from reality. It was in that moment of insanity that she felt she had to shoot Mrs. Donahue. We will present a strong background and historical case that will show that Rebecca was on course for a mental breakdown long before that fateful day. At the end of it, I trust you will find her not guilty by reason of temporary insanity. Thank you."

Is that all he had to say about why this fool had tried to kill me? With representation like that, we wouldn't be here that long after all. Surely the jury could see right through this case, it was so full of holes it was ridiculous.

Now that the opening arguments had been presented, the judge released the court for recess. We were going to reconvene at 1:00 p.m. I didn't know how much more of this I could stomach, but we all decided to have lunch and discuss what had just transpired.

Before I could get out of the courtroom, I was stopped by Lance. He looked at my husband and asked, "May I have a word with Denise, please?"

Malachi looked at me, and when I nodded, he answered "Sure." He looked at me again and said, "Baby, I'll be standing right out the door if you need me."

I shook my head. Lance motioned for me to take a seat, then said "Denise, I just want to know if you will ever forgive me for putting you through this."

I smiled at Lance and said, "You brought this burden into your life, but I'm free now, Lance. I don't know what it will take for you to get over me, but you're going to have to reexamine yourself and decide how to move on. The one thing I'm grateful for is that because all of this happened, I met that man standing outside of that door, and it's been the best thing for me."

Lance looked solemn as I spoke about my husband, then said "Even though you're not with me anymore, I'm glad you found someone who makes you happy. You were always a good girl, Denise, and from looking at you, it seems as if you trust this Malachi, which is something you said you couldn't do with me again. I'll let you go, Denise, but I just wanted you to know that I'm sorry for Rebecca hurting you, and I'm sorry for the tears that I made you shed. You didn't deserve any of this."

I thanked Lance for his words. I really wished him well, as there was no turning back the hands of time where we were concerned, but my heart went out to him.

It turns out Lance wasn't the only one who wanted to repent his sins. When we were finished speaking, Carl was standing outside with my family. Zondra took the liberty of introducing him to Malachi. Carl hugged me and said, "Denise, it's been a long time. You look good. Congratulations on your marriage." He pointed to Malachi who was now standing next to me. "Malachi here is a lucky man. Look, Niecey—I never got a chance to thank you for everything you did for me while we were back in school. I didn't know what went down with you and Rebecca until the investigator tracked me down. I'm sorry for all of that, but I wanted to come here to testify on your behalf. You've always been a good friend, and I was young and dumb way back when I hurt you. It wasn't worth it, and this shouldn't have happened to you."

I assured Carl that in some strange way, everything that happened with Rebecca had prepared me to stand next to this man I'm now married to. Carl nodded his head and extended his hand to Malachi. "My man, keep doing your job because you got a heck of a woman by your side."

Malachi said, "I plan to, partner." With that Carl walked away and we left the courthouse heading for lunch.

CHAPTER 45

We had almost two hours to kill before we had to return to court. There weren't any restaurants nearby that tempted our tummies so we had to venture out where we found an Outback Steakhouse. We had a large group. My parents, who had been unusually quiet since they arrived in Savannah; Malachi's parents; Deborah, who had come with Kevin, they'd left the kids in Miami with his parents, and Diane with David, who God bless him was now her fiancé. Then of course there was Zondra and Malcolm. Although the reason behind the gathering wasn't too joyous, it was a good feeling to have everyone together; we were alive and healthy, and that was reason enough to celebrate.

Lunch was fun. During which, I asked everyone's opinion about the opening statements from both attorneys. Zondra quickly gave her expert opinion: "The prosecutor definitely presented a good case, he was clear and concise. The defense doesn't seem to be as well prepared, but he might have a trick up his sleeve. I'm interested in knowing what he was referring to when he said that Rebecca had been rejected and denied all of her life."

I said, "I don't know, but I guess we'll find out." I looked over at my parents who had worry frowns etched across their faces, so I gave them a smile to let them know that I was fine and they didn't have to worry about me. Then Diane, always the tactless one, said, "Forget about those attorneys— Malachi, how does it feel to see so many of Denise's exes in one room?"

I was getting ready to speak on my husband's behalf when Malachi said, "No, baby—I got this one. Diane, this is my wife, the one that God chose for me. You said it right—they're exes. Everybody sitting at this table has a past, but Denise's present and future are with me. Those men messed up, and now I got her, and I guarantee you I won't ever be an ex." That made Diane shut up, and to show that he meant what he said about not becoming an ex, Malachi tilted my head and tongue kissed me right in front of everybody.

I said, "That's right, baby, I ain't going nowhere as long as you keep putting the smack down like that."

Malcolm jumped in, "That's right, bro—we're Donahue men and our women are well taken care of, ain't that right, Z? Now, Diane, too bad we don't have any other brothers otherwise you might get a chance to know what real love is." We all burst out laughing because that's what Diane gets for opening her big mouth and trying to be funny.

She said, "Forget all of you."

Just as we were almost done with lunch, Malachi received a call on his cell phone. He said, "Everyone, that was the prosecutor's office. They want to meet with us before we go back into court." I looked at Malachi, but he just shrugged his shoulders.

Zondra said, "Maybe the defense decided to take a plea deal after all." It made sense to me, so we finished our meals and prepared to return to the courthouse and listen to what the prosecutor had to tell us.

Mr. Davenport arranged for all of us meet in an office adjacent to the judge's chambers. He said that he'd wanted to take this opportunity to tell us something before the media broke the story. He said, "The trial is over." We all clapped and said thank you Jesus before we starting jumping for joy.

Then Mr. Davenport said he had some more news for us: "This isn't how I wanted this to end, but while you all were on break for lunch, there was an accident at the holding facility where Rebecca Bennett was being held."

My father stood up and asked, "What happened?" Mom stood next to him to calm him down.

Mr. Davenport went on to say, "The details are sketchy, but it appears that Rebecca committed suicide." My father let out a screech that was piercing and my mother collapsed to the floor. Everyone scrambled to console my dad and revive my mother, but I was still sitting at the table in total disbelief at what I just heard. I didn't know how I should've reacted to the news. I'd wanted her to be punished for what she did to me, but I didn't want her soul to burn in hell for taking her own life, especially since she couldn't ask for forgiveness now and was destined to spend eternity in hell.

Now for the life of me, I didn't know why my parents were taking the news so badly. If anything, I should be the one sprawled out on the ground because I felt like Rebecca got the last word again.

Mr. Davenport allowed us all to remain in the room until we were ready to depart, then added, "There will be a backlash at the prison for what happened, but apparently last night one of the guards allowed Rebecca to have a razor to shave her legs in preparation for court, and when they took it back from her, they didn't check to see if the razor was intact. She hid the razor on her person, and when court was in recess and she was led back to the holding cell, she used the belt that she was wearing to hang herself and the razor blade to cut her wrists. By the time the guards found her, it was too late. Now I think you all have some things to discuss, and I would suggest you do it before the news media gets a hold of the story, because they won't paint a pretty picture."

While my parents were pulling themselves together, I tried to understand what Mr. Davenport was talking about. What could the media tell me that I already didn't know about Rebecca Bennett, other than this just proved the point that she was definitely insane? This was just too much to absorb. If it wasn't for bad luck, I wouldn't have had any luck at all.

However, as badly as I wanted to sit right there in the middle of the floor and bawl my eyes out, I knew it was useless. Malachi stood vigil over me just to make sure that I wouldn't have another panic attack. Everyone was in a daze at the news. I mean, just a few minutes ago we'd been having lunch and laughing at each other, but now we were sitting here trying to make sense of the death of the woman who'd impacted all of our lives. My parents had got it together by now, and everyone took a seat at the table once again.

Pops said that he wanted everyone's attention for a minute, and I sat back wondering what he had to say. He began, "I want to say this because it's been eating at me for quite some time, and I don't know how my girls are going to feel about me after I say this, but it may shed some light on what Mr. Davenport was talking about regarding the news media." He looked at my mom and then took a deep breath. All of us were now sitting on the edge of our seats.

Pops continued, "A long time ago, just after Deborah was born, JoAnn and I were having a tough time in our marriage. We were fighting so much and things were hard. We'd gotten married when we were young and money was tight, then Deborah came along, and it was another mouth to feed. I guess we just didn't know how to cope. Then I did the dumbest thing in the world and decided to leave my family, and in doing so I had an affair with another woman. Now this woman sitting next to me, I love her more than words can express, and she forgave me for my indiscretion. We wanted to save our marriage, so she allowed me to come back home. Things between us got better, and everything I was worried about somehow didn't matter anymore. I promised your mother I was through with the other woman, and JoAnn never doubted me. Soon after my return we found out that we were expecting another child, and Denise is as precious to us now as she was then.

After Niecey was born, I ran into the woman I had the affair with and we struck up a conversation. That one conversation led to me sleeping with her one last time, and I say one last time because I had to face your mother and let her know that I had committed adultery for the second time in our marriage."

For once I was glad that Diane interrupted. She said, "What the hell are you telling us this for?"

Pops said, "Hold on, baby girl—let me finish. Because I had to confess to your mother that I had cheated on her, quite naturally she was upset, and I can remember what she told me as if were yesterday. She said, 'Now I forgave you once, and you went back to this woman. I've never given you a reason to bring this shame on me and these girls, but you tell me now if you're in love with this woman, I will walk out of this house and you'll never see us again. But, if you're willing to do what it takes to earn my trust and love again, then you pick up that phone right now and tell that woman that you don't want anything to do with her ever again.' After I made that telephone call, I had never seen or spoken to that woman again until recently."

Deborah had something to say now: "Now hold on a minute, you wait until all of us are grown to tell us that you cheated on Mom, and now you want to be with this woman?"

Pops said, "No, what I'm saying is that the woman I had the affair with is Rebecca Bennett's mother."

The room got so quiet until you could hear a rat pissing on a cotton ball. Diane was the brave one when she said, "Ain't that some shit." Malachi looked at me, but all I could do was shoot evil glances in my dad's direction.

Pops continued, "To make this situation even worse, after I saw Roxanne, Rebecca's mother, in the courtroom when Rebecca entered her plea, she yelled at me that this was all my fault. I didn't understand what she meant. But right after we returned home to Miami, she had the attorney contact me and your mother because she thought we should know something about her daughter.

When the attorney gave us Roxanne's information, we invited her to our home to have a conversation as adults. Roxanne apologized to your mother for disrespecting her by having an affair with me. She said she'd also had her share of troubles, and she believed that it was due to the part she had played in our affair. She then went on to say that after I called to tell her never to contact me again, she'd learned that she was pregnant, and the child she was carrying belonged to me. That child was Rebecca."

That's when I lost it. I got up and ran over to my dad and slapped him. I told him, that he was a low-down dog, and that he'd made that woman put a bullet in my chest all because he couldn't keep his dick in his pants.

Malachi told me, "Relax—you weren't there, and you don't know what happened, so it's not for you to pass judgment."

I shot him a look that he knew all too well as meaning "don't test me." Malachi backed off, asking me, "Where do we go from here?"

"I don't know where the hell they go from here, but I'm taking my black ass back to Atlanta to mind my own damn business and get the hell away from these people."

My mother-in-law got up to stop me from leaving, saying, "Denise, if for nothing else, stay to support your mom. We're all family here, and you walking out is not going to change what happened. It's in the past, and we're all going to deal with it as a family. Don't leave." Her words were enough to soothe me, but I still had so many questions running through my mind.

I might stay to support my mom, but I didn't have to like one minute of it. I guess it all made sense now. Here was another stupid man who'd been seduced by a Bennett woman. It was in Rebecca's genes all along—she got those whore qualities naturally. But I still didn't understand why her hatred was so strong against me in particular. I had two other sisters she could have tormented, so why me?

My dad began to sob once again. For all I cared, he could cry a river. This whole thing was his fault. He was another man I loved who'd been stolen away by a Bennett woman.

CHAPTER 46

Rebecca Bennett was my half sister, and I hadn't even known it. She had kept that secret all of her life. No wonder she was psychotic. It wasn't my fault. Her simple mother should have said something a long time ago and it would have saved us all some tears and me some bloodshed.

Malachi didn't know how to comfort me after Pops made his announcement. What the hell could he say? I didn't want to hear no Bible verses either. This was a lot to handle, but I was going to deal with it without having a panic attack. Time was the only thing that was going to help me put these thirty years of secrets behind me. Yeah, Pops cheated on my mom and she chose to stay with him (I don't know what she was thinking), and maybe it wasn't his fault that Rebecca's mom never told him about his illegitimate daughter, but it was still going to take some time for me to get over the entire thing.

After Pops dropped his bombshell, we all left Savannah with a cloud of despair hanging over our heads. My sisters and I talked on the phone all the time now discussing the fact that we had another sister. We all were upset with my dad, but I was the only one who hadn't spoken a word to him since we left Savannah. Deborah told me he was taking it pretty hard, and he was even thinking about stepping down as a deacon. I said, "He should—he's supposed to lead by example, and that's not an example I'd want anyone to follow."

Diane said, "Niecey, you don't have to be so hard on him. It happened a long time ago, and besides, he didn't know anything about our crazy sister." I told Diane she wasn't funny. He was our dad, and of all men I thought he was above any scandal, but he had just proven that he's a man, and none of them can be trusted.

Deborah said, "Don't bash all men, Denise. I have a good husband, and so do you, and if Diane can train David the right way, he'll be a good man for her. Pops made a huge mistake, but it's not for us to judge him." I told my sisters that I wasn't judging him—I was just extremely disappointed with him.

Deborah continued, "By the way, Denise, Rebecca's funeral is this weekend, and Mom and Dad wanted to know if you would attend."

I yelled so loud, I know I almost burst their eardrums on the other end of the phone: "How dare you ask me something like that, when that woman tried to kill me! Hell no, I'm not going to no funeral, so don't bother asking me again! You go to a funeral when you're going to miss the person who's dead, and I'm not going to miss Rebecca Bennett at all."

Diane said, "She's your sister." I hung up the phone.

Throughout the week, Malachi also tried to persuade me to go to the funeral. He said, "Denise, I know that you don't care that Rebecca is dead, but maybe you should go just to show your folks you care about them."

"I can send them a card to let them know I care. I don't have to go sit up in nobody's church and stare at Rebecca Bennett in a casket for them to know that I care about them." Matter of fact, I knew I wasn't going to sit up and pretend to mourn the loss of a great person. There was nothing great about Rebecca, and I wasn't in mourning.

There was also a lot of media attention about Rebecca's death at the prison. A couple of prison guards lost their jobs because of negligence, and once they found out the truth about my dad, it was a free-for-all. They staked out the house in Miami hoping to get an interview or a photo of my parents. Nope, I could do without all of that stuff. Rebecca always loved the limelight, and even in death she had people talking about her. It appeared this woman would haunt me until my dying days. So that was further reason why I wouldn't be in attendance at the home going services of Rebecca Bennett.

Zondra called frequently to see how I was holding up. I just wanted someone to tell me that I wasn't wrong to feel the way I did. Being the true friend and sister that she was, Zondra said, "Hell no, you're not wrong—you didn't do anything wrong and you don't owe anyone any apologies. Don't you be sitting around that house worrying yourself or my brother-in-law. What you need to do is come over to my house and we all can go out and get drunk. Well, since you're not a drinker, I'll get drunk for you, and then you can go back home and make love to your husband because I plan on breaking my man's back tonight." That girl had a way with words, with her nasty self. I told her it sounded like a great idea.

Malachi was all for going out with Zondra and his brother; he would do anything to get me out of the house. I told him he wasn't ready for what I had in store for him. He said, "Mrs. Donahue, anything you got I can handle. If you keep it up, you might be calling your girl back and telling her that we need to take a rain check because we already got started."

Either I'm too old, or we must have gone to the club on "wear your itsy-bitsy clothes night." The females in that place had on next to nothing, and I felt overdressed. Considering Zondra and I entered with not one but two identical caramel brothers who had it going on, of course all eyes would be on us, and as soon as we turned our backs, the chicken heads would be pecking their way to our men. We were going to leave, but Malachi said he wanted to stay. It was rare that we did anything like this, and we'd gotten dressed and come all the way there, we just might as well enjoy the evening. Zondra and Malcolm agreed, so we got a table and sat down.

However, Zondra wouldn't sit for too long. That girl knew she could sweat out some hair and wear out some shoes. All of us went out on the dance floor, and Lord if the people in church could only see me. It seemed like hours that we were on that dance floor. I went to the DJ to request a special song, and when Tony Terry's "With You" came on, Malachi knew that was all me. It was supposed to be our wedding song at our reception, but that changed when I got shot. When he heard the music, he grabbed me and we swayed to it. We held onto each other and got lost in the moment.

I looked him in his eyes, and he whispered that he loved me. I told him I loved him more, and we started kissing right there on the dance floor, our tongues dancing just as our bodies moved to the music. We were lost in each other until Zondra tapped me on the shoulder and said, "Excuse me, the song has been over for a while now—you two need to get a room."

I told her I agreed with her and said "Bye." My man and me left to do like R. Kelly's song suggests, *go half on a baby*.

CHAPTER 47

The cliché that time heals all wounds is very true. It took some time, but I truly forgave Pops for his mistake. What happened with him and Roxanne was a long time ago. I had just been taking my anger out on him because I didn't have a chance to let Rebecca see that she might have wounded me, but she didn't kill my spirit. However, she killed herself before I had a chance to confront her, and my anger was redirected to my dad instead.

I apologized for disrespecting him, and he asked for my forgiveness for being such a fool and causing me to get shot. Of course I forgave him. Something had been taken away from him, and he had a daughter that he never got the chance to know. I told him not to blame himself for Rebecca. He hadn't known she existed, and I was sorry she didn't get a chance to experience the love he showered on me and my sisters.

My mom even got on the telephone to share some of her thoughts with me. She told me that when I was going through the divorce with Lance, she wasn't trying to give me any bad advice. All she'd wanted to do was to let me know that you can't run every time trouble comes your way—you have to be prepared to stand and defend what's important to you. I told her I understood how she felt, but those are her convictions based on what was going on in her life at the time. I told her, "Maybe you would have thought differently about taking Daddy back if you actually caught him in the act." It's a sight I couldn't get out of my mind, and it wouldn't be right to live with someone I didn't trust and couldn't stand the sight of.

My mom appreciated my honesty. I told her I understood that she loved my dad and that she was willing to save her family no matter what. She told me she loved the Lord more than anything, and it's the only thing that helped her through that period in her life when she didn't have anyone else to lean on. God supported her in one of her most trying times, and his word is what she turned to when she didn't know where else to go.

Mom also told me that she was sorry for intruding in my business when Malachi and I became a couple. She said she had no right to stick her nose in my affairs, and that although she really liked Lance and thought things could have worked out if I hadn't been so stubborn, she really loved Malachi.

He had proven himself to be a good, honest, God-fearing man who was set on leading his family in the right direction. "I'm so proud to call him my son, Denise, and I can see that he makes you beam with happiness. You just keep doing whatever it is you're doing, because together you all can conquer anything."

I was so full of pride. It felt great to hear my mother acknowledge my husband for all that he is to me. I couldn't wait until Malachi got home to tell him what she'd said about him. I liked the change that was taking place in this family. God had been good to me, and he kept right on blessing me. Just when I thought I was on the brink of disaster or a breakdown, he stepped right in and showed his love. Everything that had occurred over the past few months would be enough to send the average person over the edge, but instead I thought of Numbers 6:26 in the Bible that helped me to understand God's grace and mercy:

May the Lord show you his favor and give you his peace.

CHAPTER 48

Love definitely was in the air, especially as my little sister had decided on a fall wedding date. She was finally going to marry her long-time boyfriend David. My dad was excited because this was the last Martin girl to walk down the aisle. From what I knew of his youngest daughter, this would be an event to remember: this child did everything on a grand scale, and since she knew so many people, she pulled one of Star Jones's numbers and got her wedding done with little to no out-of-pocket expense to my parents. That girl definitely knew how to work her looks and charm. I guess a pretty face and a big ass did go a long way.

My little sister never ceased to amaze me—not only did she get her wedding paid for, but she managed to have the event televised. Only Diane Martin could pull off a stunt of this magnitude.

She had telephone conferences with me to let me know that I better be on point when I stood at her wedding. In particular, she mentioned she was giving Deborah and me ample time to get our bodies together because the television camera adds pounds. That witch had some nerve—I'll be glad when she has a baby and her hips and thighs spread like biscuits. Besides I didn't know what she was talking about. Hell, I worked out every day and I was still fine, so she couldn't have been directing her comments towards me.

All of this television stuff had come about because the company she is contracted with wanted to do something that would boost its revenue. Diane is a model commentator at fashion shows; the company she works with regularly thought it would be a fabulous idea to showcase some original creations at her wedding. It didn't take much to persuade Diane—once she heard the word *television*, I'm sure all she saw was the Hollywood lights, and she was sold.

Before long the wedding turned into a circus. I asked Diane what David had to say about this fiasco. She replied, "Just 'yes, dear'—see I'm getting him trained just like you and Deborah suggested. He's catching on quick, huh?"

I told her, "Very funny, Diane, but it's his day also and he should have a say so in how things are going to go."

All Diane had to say was, "Be quiet, Niecey—I can't help it if you and Deborah don't like the finer things in life. I can't be content with the simple life."

"Don't get me started. You better wake up and get a clue, because when you realize that beauty fades, you better have something else that's more valuable than material things to fall back on, because no man wants a woman who doesn't think about anything except how she looks."

I couldn't faze that girl, she came back with, "Huh, that's what you think—look at Kimora Lee Simmons." I hung up the phone realizing I just couldn't get through to her.

The wedding was now slated for production in three months. I would be there for my sister, but I wasn't sure how much she was doing this for television instead of for love. David was a nice guy, and he had a good business mind. I thought Diane would calm down when he put a ring on her finger, but it had taken a two-year engagement before he was able to back her into a corner and pinpoint an exact date for their nuptials. I always thought he was the perfect balance for Diane—she was the wild and crazy one while he was calm and cool. He had to be that way, because if both of them had egos like hers, somebody would get strangled. If he could put up with it her and her antics, then God bless him.

Extravagant doesn't even begin to describe their wedding. I'd never seen anything like it before in my life. When everyone was ready for the wedding to begin, I was busy teasing Malachi and Malcolm. They were groomsmen, and I wanted to know how they felt about their television debut. They were so handsome and debonair, I told them, "You could have a new career after this by becoming the new Doublemint twins." They didn't find my comments amusing especially since they were nervous about standing up in front of so many people.

Before we were scheduled to take our places, Malachi called for me to meet him in the hallway. He told me that no one knew where David was, and they hadn't seen him since the bachelor party the night before. "Did you check his room?" I asked.

"David checked out of the hotel early this morning. We've been trying to reach him on his cell phone, but apparently he's not answering."

We had to find him before Diane realized that something was wrong and before the cameras started rolling. But looking for David turned out to be extremely difficult and we didn't know where to start. I didn't know what to tell my sister. She was so excited about her special day—how could I tell her that her fiancé was missing in action?

Malachi and Malcolm said that when they found David, they wanted to beat the crap out of him for what he was doing to Diane. "What good would that do?" I asked my husband. "Besides, we don't know what's going on. Let's wait until we hear something before you start talking about beating anyone up."

Just as Malachi and Malcolm were calming down, my husband got a call on his cell phone. It was David. Malachi put it on speaker so Malcolm and I could hear him say that he'd just called to let everyone know why he wasn't at his own wedding.

Malachi told him that he needed to be a man and come and explain himself to Diane, which was the least that he could do. David said he couldn't face Diane right now because she wouldn't understand how he felt. Malachi did his best to persuade David to carry through with his commitment.

By this time, the producers of the show were asking for everyone to get in position before the cameras started rolling. I didn't think I had the heart to tell Diane that her man had stood her up, but someone had to do it. Before I went in to speak with my sister, David said he wanted to talk to Diane. I took the phone away from Malachi and I went into the dressing room to face her.

She was standing in front of the mirror admiring herself, then she turned to me and asked, "Do you think David will like my dress?" Obviously she could tell something was wrong by the expression on my face. I just held the phone out to her and said, "It's for you."

CHAPTER 49

There was no storybook wedding for my sister Diane. She tried to hold up a brave front when she told us that David didn't want to marry her. He'd said he wanted a wife who was more attracted to him than the limelight. Never one to be at a loss for words, Diane told him, "I think you could have told me that before you agreed to get married on live television and humiliate me." David told her that he didn't expect for her to understand, but that he just knew how he felt, and he couldn't marry her unless she was truly committed to having a lasting relationship with him.

A small part of me admired my baby sister for how she handled the entire situation, but I also understood how David felt. She politely told David that they had been dating for the past five years and he knew her better than anyone. He had numerous opportunities to back out of the relationship, but instead he waited until the day of her wedding in front of all her family, friends, and colleagues to degrade her in the most unforgiving manner. Then she said she had to a plane to catch and she was going to enjoy the tickets to Mexico that his parents had sprung for. With that Diane hung up the telephone and cried in my arms.

This was not a moment for "I told you so"; Diane was already feeling really low. I didn't want her to have to explain this to her guests, so I told her to do what she needed to and I would let everyone know there wasn't going to be a wedding. Malachi went with me, I had to find the television producer and explain the situation to him. Needless to say, he wasn't thrilled at the announcement because several top designers had invested time and money into having their garments showcased on national television. He also advised me that my sister would be ruined in this industry, she couldn't just back out of a contract without repercussions. When I asked him if there was anything we could do to save her reputation, he looked at me and said, "The show must go on." I couldn't argue with him on that one. I looked at Malachi and shrugged my shoulders, and he said, "The things I do for love."

It wasn't hard to persuade everyone to participate in the fashion show since it was to preserve Diane's good name, although she herself had hightailed it out of the building. Deborah and I had to gather up all of the wedding party and make them wait on instructions from the event coordinator. My parents wanted to go and see about their baby, but I reassured them that this was one time Diane needed to handle things on her own. She was a big girl, and she had to deal with her own mess; besides she didn't want anyone all up in her business. If I knew my sister—and I think I knew her all too well— she was on her way to the airport thinking about which bikini she was going to lay out in and how she would find her a man in Mexico to soothe her pain.

The fashion show went off without a hitch, and the producers told me I might have just salvaged my sister's career. After the show was over, we continued the festivities; the food was already paid for, it made no sense to waste it.

Diane called from the airport to ask me how everyone took the news. I told her she owed us all a big favor because we'd just saved her behind from being blackballed in the industry. She said, "Thanks, big sis. Let Mom and Dad know that I'm OK. I just need this time to figure out what my next move is."

I told her, "Take your time—it's not like you have a man to rush home to." Diane laughed at my joke, and I knew she would be just fine.

CHAPTER 50

Being stood up at her wedding made Diane take a long hard look at herself. When she returned home from Mexico, she called me and asked what I thought about her opening a boutique. I said, "How much of that tainted water in Mexico did you drink? What kind of scheme are you thinking of now?"

Diane said, "I know you all think that I don't care about anything except how I look. Now don't get me wrong—appearance isn't everything, but I just happen to take a strong interest in my outer shell, and I think others would like to do the same thing. Besides fashion has been a profitable business for me. It's just that I think it is time to redirect my attention to some other business interests, and I just wanted to see how you felt about it because I value your opinion."

Hmmm, my sister was talking to me about what she should do with her life. I asked her, "What, have you had enough of the fabulosity? Are you now interested in the simple life like me and Deborah?"

She laughed and said, "OK, I deserve that one. I apologize for what I said about you and Deborah's lives."

"Apology accepted—now let's decide what we're going to name this boutique."

Having a lawyer as a sister-in-law and best friend really came in handy when trying to develop a business plan for Diane's ideas. Zondra knew so many people that it wasn't difficult for her to put Diane in contact with someone who would help her. Diane loved fashion and everything it involved; she wanted to create a store that would offer clothing resembling what the popular designers were making for models to walk the runway in Paris or Milan. Her boutique would cater to the every whim of women who had caviar taste on a fish stick budget. Many of the designers she knew were looking for a way to get their designs noticed, Diane offered an opportunity that was hard to resist. Diane was all business as she decided what garments would be showcased in her store, how her display cases would be arranged, and where the mannequins would be displayed. Soon she was interviewing potential employees. She was dedicated to making her boutique a reality.

It took close to a year for Diane to pick an ideal location, she wanted LMS Creations to be the most talked-about fashion store in all of Miami. Finally her grand opening was just three weeks away, and Malachi and I were going down to Miami to help her celebrate. There was just something about that city that caused you to never get bored living there. Although I hated when it was too busy and congested with traffic and tourists, Dorothy knew what she was talking about in *The Wizard of Oz* when she said, "There's no place like home."

Malachi and I were staying at my parents' home while we were in town; I figured that we could tolerate them for the weekend. Everyone was excited about Diane's grand opening, but she was a nervous wreck; she'd invited so many guests, hoping that her shop would be a success.

The night before the big opening tomorrow morning, Diane had to put the finishing touches on her store so Deborah and I decided to give her a hand. While in the shop, we told Diane that we would never have thought she was capable of pulling something of this magnitude off without it turning into a disaster. She said, "What are ya'll trying to do, jinx me?"

I told her, "Girl, we're just joking with you—relax. By the way, what the hell does 'LMS Creations' stand for?"

"I would have told you, but since you are acting funky with me, you'll just have to wait until tomorrow and listen to the announcement I make before we open."

Finally the moment had arrived, and the entire family including Zondra and Malcolm were standing outside the doors sweating bullets. It was 9:30 a.m. and already hot as hell. I didn't want to be all day long waiting on this girl, but she wouldn't be Diane if she didn't make a grand entrance. Just when I was about to call her, she arrived in a pearl white chauffeur-driven Mercedes Benz. This damn girl never quit. I just shook my head at her.

When she got out of the car, she strode up to the front door like she was working the runway, then said, "I would like to thank you all for coming out to celebrate the Grand Opening of Love My Sisters Creations, I hope that LMS will give you that look you've been searching for at a cost that doesn't hurt your pockets. I've put a lot of blood, sweat, tears, and money into this project and I want every woman to feel as if she's a different person when she wears something from my store. But before I open the doors, I would like my daddy to say a prayer for the success of my business."

Pops came up to the front of the store and said, "Father God, we come here today to support Diane as she embarks upon a new adventure in her life. Lord, you have guided her all the way, and it is my prayer that through all of her hard work that she will prosper. As she prospers, Lord, let her remember that as long as she seeks you in all that she does, she will succeed. These and all blessings we ask in your son Jesus name. Amen. "

Then Diane opened the doors and the customers rushed in. As her family, we assisted when necessary. At a break, Zondra, Deborah, and me took Diane to the back of the store. We all gave her a big hug and told her how proud of her we were. We also told her that naming her store after us was the best present she could have given us, so now we wanted to give her something special. We held out a box for Diane. When she opened it, she found a diamond nameplate that read *LMS*. She was happy about our gift to her and said she would always wear it.

When we went back into the store, it turned out Diane had another surprise waiting for her. In the middle of the store surrounded by Malachi and Malcolm, David stood with a big bouquet of flowers in his hand. He said to Diane, "Can we talk?"

CHAPTER 51

Who knew that Diane's former fiancée would show up at her grand opening? David looked real good, and while my husband and brother-in-law were giving him the "You better not mess with our sister" stare down, Diane went right on assisting her customers just like David being in the room didn't faze her at all. She was cold as ice, but I could tell that it was just a front to mask her nervousness about David being here.

I went over to David and asked him what he wanted. He told me he had been trying to get in contact with Diane for well over four months, but she had ignored all of his calls. Then he'd read about the opening of her boutique in the business section of the newspaper and wanted to come down here and face her. At least he thought that way she couldn't ignore him, but now he knew that Diane could walk right past him as if he were a stranger on the street.

When I told David that maybe this wasn't such a good idea for him to be in the store, Malachi jumped in with a "Yeah!"

I told him, "Be quiet—I don't need any backup on this song." I knew Malachi was upset with David for running out on Diane on their wedding day and that he thought the way David handled things was cowardly and disrespectful. I agreed with my husband, but David had to live with his actions, not us. The way Malachi was standing by, he was acting as if he and his brother were going to beat the man down in the store in front of all these witnesses.

Before my man ended up back in jail for defending my little sister's honor, I told David, "Maybe you should return later, just before the store closes." David wanted to protest, but he saw my back up and thought it would be better to leave the premises.

After he was gone, I turned around to Malachi and called him a big bully. He just grinned and said, "I wasn't going to bother with that knucklehead—I just wanted to let him know that if he wanted to be a part of this family, then he should know the men in it act like men. That's why our wives are submissive like they're supposed to be." I punched him in the chest and he patted me on my behind.

Helping Diane out in the boutique was exhausting work, and by closing time, I was wiped out. My parents had left earlier in the afternoon, so had Deborah-she needed to get back to her beauty salon. Taking advantage of the Florida weather, my husband and his brother decided to go play golf. Kevin had to go home to watch my niece and nephews until Deborah made it home from her salon.

That left Zondra and me to stay behind and assist Diane with everything from ringing up customers at the cash register to getting the appropriate sizes for customers when the clothes were up high on the racks or we had to run to the storeroom to keep garments on the shelves. I had to keep a smile on face all day long so my cheeks were tired. Diane said that we could leave and she would remain behind with her employees to clean up and prepare for tomorrow's sales. I hugged her and told her I was so proud of her and that I thought she'd done a spectacular job with the boutique.

Zondra was just as tired as I was as well and hungry, so we called our husbands and decided to meet them at the IHOP for dinner. We were having a great time, Zondra and I teased our husbands about the suntan they'd received while out on the golf course. Their skin was sensitive to the touch, and both just wanted to lie down and rest before we got on the road and returned to Atlanta tomorrow. It didn't bother me one bit because I could sleep until next week after being on my feet all day long helping Diane. As Zondra and Malcolm said good night, they reminded me that they would see us at my parents' house tomorrow for breakfast.

Malachi and I left the parking lot of the IHOP, I could have sworn I saw a familiar face drive past, but then again, I could have just been so tired that I was seeing things.

However, while I might have been tired the night before, the next morning I was well rested and knew I hadn't been delirious the night before about who I'd seen. As everyone gathered at my parents' house for breakfast, Diane showed up with David in the same car that had driven past us in the parking lot. This girl had some explaining to do; she couldn't expect to just waltz in here with this man like everything was hunky-dory.

Everyone was waiting to hear how it came to be that they were here together and why. Diane should have known she wasn't going to be able to sit at this table and deflect all of the stares and glares we were sending her way. When someone finally spoke, it wasn't Diane but David. He stood up and said, "I have something I want to say to everyone gathered here. It's been a long time since I've seen you all, and I think I owe you all an apology and an explanation as to why I couldn't marry Diane on our wedding day.

Mr. and Mrs. Martin, you all have always been good to me, and I really appreciate you inviting me into your family as if I was one of your own children. To the rest of you who may think that what I did was spineless and heartless, I want to ask for your forgiveness for what happened that day. As for you, Diane, I know that we talked last night and I explained myself to you, but I want to say this again in front of everyone.

Things between us were going well, but then all of a sudden I felt as if I was just a pawn in your chess game. I didn't feel as if you included me in any decisions that you made—it was as if you acted upon your own intuition and never gave a thought as to what I felt about a certain situation. I no longer felt as if I had a say so in anything that was planned for our benefit. Even when 'we' were planning 'our' wedding, I saw things just spiraling out of control, and I couldn't reel you back in. I just couldn't live my life like that, so I didn't show up. Not going through with that day has pained my heart over the months, but I can't help the way I felt, and I couldn't go into a marriage knowing that my wife preferred the glamorous life as opposed to being my helpmate.

When I found out you were opening a store, I had to take a chance at explaining myself to you face to face. I've been missing you so much, and I stand here today as a man confessing and professing my love for you, woman. I want you back, and I'm begging for your forgiveness and asking that you take me back."

Deborah, Zondra, and I were all crying at David's words. My dad went over to David and shook his hand, then said, "It takes a big man to admit when he's wrong, but it takes a bigger person to do it front of all these women and have them crying like this. You're alright with me, son." All the other men at the table got up and shook David's hand.

When we were all seated again with our tears wiped away; David looked at Diane and asked, "Will you have me back Diane?"

Diane looked up at him and said, "Man, you had me yesterday when you walked into the boutique." We all laughed at that crazy girl and asked them what's next.

David said, "I want to marry this woman, and I'm not walking out this time."

"Oh, we know that because there wouldn't be a rock on earth that you would be able to hide under to get away from us," Malachi told him.

Malcolm chimed in, "That's right."

CHAPTER 52

We could tell David's impressive return was what Diane had needed. Her demeanor had changed overnight and she didn't have anything flippant to say for the remainder of the morning. Sitting around with the family was so relaxing to me; matter of fact, it was too relaxing and I just knew something was on the brink of killing the positive vibes that were in the air. My intuitions never failed me, and I had a gut feeling that things were about to get hectic.

Instinctively, Malachi could sense that something was bothering me. All the women cleared the table and the men moved to the entertainment room, Malachi stayed behind for a moment to rub my back and nuzzle my neck playfully to distract my thoughts. He always knew just what to do to keep me from worrying about everything.

My gut feeling never disappointed me, so when the doorbell rang, I didn't leave the kitchen area to see who was at the door. It was Diane who answered the door, and she summoned my parents. I could hear the voices that were now coming from the living room. Malachi returned to the kitchen and asked me to come join the rest of the family.

The person at the door was Rebecca's mother, Ms. Roxanne Bennett. I hadn't had a chance to really meet her, and now that she was standing in front of me, she wasn't much to look at. As a matter of fact, she was downright ugly. I'm not just saying that because her schizoid daughter attempted to kill me or because she herself had an affair with my dad—I really thought this woman had gotten beat with an ugly stick. I don't know what Pops was thinking when he messed around with her. She had the biggest head I've ever seen on a human being, not to mention lips that could give Jay-Z a run for his money. With her knocked knees, she was a natural Hot Mess! All I could do to keep myself from looking at this woman with disgust was to brace myself against my husband. He had his arm around my shoulder as we waited for an explanation for Ms. Roxanne's intrusion on our breakfast.

It was my mom who asked Ms. Roxanne to have a seat and offered her something to drink. She declined my Mom's offer of refreshments and said that she wasn't going to stay long. She said that she had spent a long time on her knees praying to God for guidance and the strength to come over here and make a desperate plea to our family. She said that she had exhausted all of her avenues looking for a solution, and she wanted to let us know what her plans for the future were before she left the state.

My sisters and I all gave one another "the eye," and I knew we were thinking the same thing: why does this woman think that we would care about her future endeavors? Ms. Roxanne continued, "It's been difficult for me in the past few years, having to cope with Rebecca and raising her children while she was incarcerated. Life wasn't easy when I was raising my only child alone, but I did the best that I could without help from anyone." After that comment, she looked at Pops and Mom regretfully.

"Maybe it was my fault Rebecca turned out the way she did, because I denied her the opportunity to build a relationship with her father, and I know deep down inside that Rebecca blamed me for that. Maybe I should never have told Rebecca who her biological father was or that he made the decision to stay with his family so there was no need for us to expect anything from him. I just wanted her to understand that we had to make the best out of a bad situation."

My mom interjected, "You had no right to make such a decision because we all lost so much in the end. Yes, what you and my husband did was wrong, but the child conceived out of your indiscretion was blameless. You were wrong to make the decision for us and not allow that child to know her father or her sisters."

Ms. Roxanne said, "I know what I did was wrong and selfish—that's why I'm here now. I'm hoping and praying I can be redeemed by the favor I want to ask of you and your family." Everyone in the room just looked at each other, wondering what the real reason behind Ms. Roxanne's visit was.

Before Ms. Roxanne could utter another word, there was a knock at the door. Malcolm answered the door and the cutest little boy was standing there. He said, "Mister, is my grandma finished? She told me to stay in the car, but it's kind of hot, and I have to use the bathroom."

Malcolm ushered the little fellow into the living room, then bent down to look the little boy in the eye. "Sorry, young man—I didn't catch your name."

The boy extended his hand to Malcolm and said, "It's Samuel James Bennett, but my granny calls me SJ for short." We were all shocked and impressed with the young man's introduction of himself while his grandmother sat on the couch beaming with pride.

Kevin called for his boys to come out of the other room and told them to show SJ to the restroom, then go back in the room and play video games with him. My nephews complied, and SJ seemed to think coming in from the heat was the best idea he'd ever had.

When the boys left the room, Ms. Roxanne said, "I'm so proud of him. That's why leaving him will be one of the hardest things I've ever done in my life."

Zondra was the first one to speak. "Excuse me—what do you mean by leaving him?"

Ms. Roxanne looked as if tears were about to flow from her eyes, and her big ole lips began to quiver when she said, "That's why I came over today. I wanted to let you all know that I was leaving Miami and taking Kristal, Rebecca's daughter, with me to Texas. I've raised Kristal every since Rebecca gave to birth to her while she was in high school, so I'm the only true mother she knows. Kristal is almost finished with high school, and she's at an age where she understands what is going on, and being here after what her mother did has been difficult for her. She's been withdrawn since we buried her mother. By moving us to Texas, I hope to give her a fresh start and a chance to have a normal life. Her father also lives in Texas so she'll have all of the support she needs to cope with everything that has been going on the past few years."

Zondra was not finished with her interrogation. "So what do you plan on doing with SJ?"

"As I said before, it's been extremely difficult after the passing of Rebecca, and I can't give my all to both children. I also can't teach SJ how to be a man in this world. He's a smart little boy, and since his mother's death, I'm the only parental figure he knows. His father terminated his parental rights just after SJ was born, and truthfully speaking, Rebecca was not mentally stable to love and provide for him as a mother should."

Now Diane got started as she asked, "So what do you want from us?"

"I was hoping that by giving you a chance to meet him, one of you all would offer to raise him as your own."

My mouth nearly hit the floor. I walked out of the room with Malachi fast on my heels following me into the kitchen. I could hear Deborah and Diane speak in unison when they said, "Lady, you've got to be joking." I don't know what else Ms. Roxanne said, and I really didn't care. All I knew was that the woman had some nerve to try and dump this kid off on us after everything her daughter put us through.

It was an hour before I heard Ms. Roxanne call for her grandson to come out of the room and get ready to leave. Once she was out of the door, Zondra and Malcolm came into the kitchen where Malachi and I were sitting. Zondra said, "Denise, you should come back into the living room to finish the family discussion."

I said, "I don't want to hear anything about what that woman was suggesting. I had nothing to do with the mess Pops created because he couldn't resist temptation. That's his grandchild, and he and Mom can do what they want to do without my input."

Malachi asked his brother and Zondra to leave the kitchen so that he could speak with me alone. I sat at the table with my arms crossed like a child about to have a temper tantrum. Malachi, looked at me and said, "Denise Donahue, I'm going to say this one time and one time only—you will get yourself out of this chair and go in there with your family to make a decision about the future of that little boy."

Before I could utter a word in protest, Malachi grabbed me up out of the chair and said, "I'm not asking you, I'm telling you to get up. I'm tired of this pity party that you keep throwing for yourself every time someone mentions Rebecca's name. Yeah, she shot you, but you weren't the only one that the bullet penetrated. You may have the scar on the outside, but honey, I was there that day also, and so was everyone else in this house. As your husband, I'm telling you to let it go. We have so much to be thankful for, yet you can't get over the fact that you got shot. Baby doll, she's dead and you can't allow her to continue to affect your life."

I asked Malachi, "How can I get over what happened to me when just as I start to think that my life is somewhat normal, something pops up that has Rebecca's name written all over it and just brings me back to the day she tried to kill me?"

"That's just it, Niecey—you didn't die. You are standing here in the flesh as a testament of God's good grace. It's Rebecca who is no longer with us, yet you won't let her die. I don't know what else to say or do to let you know that I love you, but your refusal to lay Rebecca to rest is threatening our future together, and I don't know how much more I can take."

I had never heard Malachi speak in such a manner, and his words stung me. I left him standing in the kitchen as I went into the living room to hear what my family had to say about Ms. Roxanne's request.

CHAPTER 53

It turned out that Ms. Roxanne was serious about not taking SJ to Texas with her and Kristal. She explained to my parents that it wasn't that she didn't love him, but that she felt guilty for depriving Rebecca of knowing her father and felt as if SJ could benefit from being raised in our family. He was seven years old, and she'd thought that now was the perfect opportunity for her to give him the opportunity to meet the family and bond with us before she relocated to Texas in four months.

I just sat and listened to my dad explain what had just transpired. He and my Mom had agreed that Samuel James should get to know our side of the family, but they felt they were too old to care for a boy his age. My dad looked at my sisters and me for a suggestion, Deborah and Diane conveniently found something on their shoes that was more interesting to look at. Then Pops said, "I suggest that one of the girls take him and raise him."

Diane quickly protested. "There's no way that I can do it. I'm sorry—I just opened LMS, and I'm not capable of raising a child right now."

David spoke up next. "As much as I would love to have him, I have to agree with Diane on this one. We haven't even set a wedding date. Plus this child is going to need lots of attention when he leaves his grandmother, and I don't think we're equipped emotionally to handle what will undoubtedly be a huge adjustment for him."

Hearing David must have given Kevin some courage he started singing the same song when he said, "I don't think we can do it either. Diamond is a toddler, the twins are teenagers, and Deborah's work is hectic. Things are tight already, and having another mouth to feed just won't work right now."

My dad put his hands in his pockets. "I'm not saying that it won't be a stressful time for all of us, but your mom and I just aren't as young as we used to be. Now we can help out with childcare and other expenses from time to time, but this child needs some young parents who can give him the love and attention he deserves."

Before my dad could get another word out, I said, "I'll take him."

Malachi had been standing in the foyer by this time, but he came over to stand next to me and said, "No, *we'll* take him." Mom started to cry and she walked over to Malachi and thanked him. Everyone else was standing around looking at me as if I were high.

Zondra asked, "Are you sure that's what you want to do?" I assured her that it was. She said, "If you're going to do this, then we're going to do it the right way. Let me make a few calls so that we can draw up adoption papers to make this legal."

I turned to Malachi and said, "There's no turning back now." "For better or for worse, I'm with you all the way, baby."

We had to share the news with Ms. Roxanne, and she was relieved that we had decided to accept SJ into our family. She wanted to explain the situation to SJ before any definite plans were made, and I told her that would be fine, we had some time before she left Miami. Besides, I had to prepare my home to suit a little person. In the meantime, it was decided that he would spend some time with my parents, and every other weekend for the next four months, Malachi and I would come down to Miami to visit with him so that he would get used to us, which would also prepare him for his move to Atlanta.

This had turned out to be quite a weekend. First we'd come to Miami to celebrate the grand opening of Diane's boutique, and then David surprised everyone by proposing to Diane at breakfast in front of the entire family. Now Malachi and I were going to be the proud parents of a seven-year-old boy whose mother was the illegitimate daughter of my dad because of an affair he had while married to my mother. Jerry Springer would definitely be interested in this story. Too bad we weren't eager to have our fifteen minutes of fame or make complete fools out of ourselves on national television; this story would truly boost his ratings.

As we traveled back to Atlanta with Zondra and Malcolm in the car, I had time to absorb the gravity of my decision. I was beginning to doubt it when my husband said, "Niecey, the moment you stepped up to say that we would take Samuel, you really reminded me of why I fell in love with you,. He's family, and it wouldn't be right for him to go into foster care when he has family who are capable of showering him with all the love and attention a child needs. Besides, he has a right to know about his lineage. The way he was born wasn't his fault, and we're going to make sure he is well taken care of."

My husband was really getting excited about becoming a father. Zondra and Malcolm teased us by saying that at least I didn't have to experience morning sickness, that I had missed the terrible twos, and that I should be grateful SJ was out of diapers. Having them joke about the situation made me relax a little, but I prayed to God and asked him for understanding as I embarked upon this journey. I was thankful I didn't have to do it alone. My husband was a real stand-up man, and even though I'm hardheaded, I know that he was sure about the path God had designed for our lives, and that it was no accident SJ had come into our lives.

I sat in the car, my fears wanted to take over and get the best of me, I felt an indescribable calm wash over me, and I could hear a faint whisper, "This is my gift to you." I knew that accepting SJ wouldn't replace the child I had lost, but hearing the voice of God gave me the confidence and reassurance I needed to become a good mother to my new son. I realized it didn't matter how Samuel James had arrived in our lives, the important thing was that he was here now, and that I have faith that everything will work our fine.

CHAPTER 54

Four months isn't long enough to prepare for a new addition to the family, but it was all the time I had to work with to get everything ready for Samuel James to come and live with us. All I have are sisters; I had no clue as to what to do with a boy, let alone a seven-year-old. I redecorated one of the spare bedrooms with everything I thought a little boy might enjoy. Malachi even got in on the decorating; he helped paint and pick out bedroom furniture he thought would suit SJ.

All we had was one more month before SJ would be with us for good. During our visits to Miami, he easily relaxed when he was around us. He played football with Malachi in my parents' backyard and talked with me about how much he liked school and how excited he would be to make new friends when he moved to Atlanta.

Before Malachi and I ended one of our visits, we thought it necessary to have a conversation with SJ and explain everything to him. We didn't want him to feel as if he wasn't wanted or that we were ripping him away from his grandmother.

Malachi and I took SJ to Pizza Hut one evening and told him we needed to have a big talk with him. Always easygoing, SJ said "Alright."

Once our pizza arrived, Malachi started by asking, "SJ, do you understand why you're coming to live with me and Aunt Denise in Atlanta?"

While shoving a slice in his mouth, SJ said, "Yes sir—my granny already explained everything to me."

Malachi and I looked at each other, and I said, "What did your grandmother tell you?"

SJ put his pizza on his plate and looked from Malachi to me. "Grandma told me that she couldn't take care of me any more, but she loved me more than anything in this world. She said that her and Kristal were going to move to Texas, and I could come and visit them if it was alright with you, but she said that my momma was real sick before she died and she didn't want me to grow up without a mommy and daddy, so she asked if you all would keep me."

I couldn't believe what was coming out of this child's mouth. I asked him, "Do you understand what your grandmother was telling you?"

He looked up at me and nodded. "Yes, it means now I have a real mommy and daddy." Malachi and I were both speechless—this child was something else. Ms. Roxanne had definitely done a fabulous job with him thus far, but I couldn't have felt any more proud if I'd given birth to him myself.

I told SJ, "Malachi and I are going to do the best job we can. You're a smart little boy, and we're happy you're coming to live with us." Then he suddenly did something that both shocked and surprised me: he got up from the table, walked over to me, and kissed me on the cheek, then he gave Malachi a big hug. This act sealed the deal with us and SJ, from that moment, he had our hearts. I couldn't wait until the end of the month when we would take him home with us for good.

Everything was all set. The adoption papers were ready; all we had to do was sign them and have the judge declare the adoption official. All parties were in agreement about the adoption, the attorney Zondra had found for us guaranteed us that everything was in accordance with the law and we were well on our way to becoming parents to Samuel James.

My sister Diane called me on the evening before we were to officially adopt SJ. She said she had something on her mind that she wanted to ask me. "Niecey, I know you're doing the noble thing by taking this kid, but don't you think that with Rebecca being his mother, that some of her craziness might rub off on him? Maybe it's just a matter of time before the psycho part shows up and he demonstrates what is undoubtedly in his blood. This thing reminds me of the movie *The Bad Seed*, and I'm afraid for you."

I told her not to worry about me, adding, "No, I don't think that SJ has inherited any of the qualities or characteristics from Rebecca that would cause Malachi and me to be alarmed for our safety."

She said, "Well as long as you're sure, then I'm there if you need me."

"Thank you, Auntie Diane—I'll remember that when Malachi and I need someone to watch SJ over the summer break." She quickly hung up the phone.

CHAPTER 55

The actual adoption proceedings lasted less than thirty minutes. All the judge did was confirm that everyone was in agreement, he then declared Samuel James to be officially adopted. We had to wait on the paperwork to be signed to legally change his name; he would now be known as Samuel James Donahue.

It was just amazing. Everyone was excited for us. Even Ms. Roxanne and SJ's sister Kristal were in attendance to say their good-byes before they left for Texas and we returned to Atlanta. I reassured them that they could call and come visit SJ whenever they wanted to. Malachi couldn't wait to get SJ back to Atlanta and start officially being a father. I can't explain the feeling that came over me when we walked out of the courthouse with SJ headed to the airport to go home. I knew that this little boy would forever change our lives, and I was grateful for his existence.

The day must have been pretty exhausting for SJ because once the plane was up in the air, he was knocked out cold. He didn't wake up until we landed in Atlanta, but then he was full of energy. When we got off the airplane, we were greeted in baggage claim by Zondra, Malcolm, and Malachi's parents. They held signs and balloons that read, "Welcome to the Family, SJ."

Samuel was surprised and asked, "Is this my family also?"

I told him, "Yes, it is."

"Cool", he replied.

Mr. and Mrs. Donahue were excited about their new grandson. They said they'd prepared a family meal that they wanted us to attend after we'd gotten SJ to our house and showed him around. Malachi told his parents that we would indeed come out to their house for dinner.

My mother-in-law never disappointed when she put together a family gathering. She'd prepared so much food in honor of SJ's homecoming that his eyes were as big as saucers from everything that was spread out on the table.

Once everyone was seated, Mr. Donahue made a toast: "Today we celebrate the arrival of a new family member, my grandson SJ. You are just what we needed around here. You have been blessed with great parents, and I pray that they will remember this moment for the rest of their lives. You are now a Donahue man, and we will raise you to be the best man that you can possibly be."

We all clapped, then SJ stood on his chair and said, "I have something I want to say also. I'm glad I have a new mommy and a daddy. This is the best day of my life, and I'm glad my name is Samuel James Donahue." With that, we all just looked at each other, then applauded.

After dinner, Zondra, Mrs. Donahue, and I cleared the table while the men sat on the patio with SJ. Both women commented that SJ seemed like an old spirit. Zondra kissed me and said, "Denise, I'm so glad that adopting SJ has made you happy. To look at all of you together, one would think that you and Malachi are his natural parents because you all look so much alike."

I hugged my friend and told her, "Thank you for all that you've done to make me a mother. It has been my heart's desire ever since I married Malachi, and you had a tremendous hand in giving me this gift. Thank you for always being in my corner and being the best girlfriend that anyone could ask for. I love you, girl, and I don't think that I could ever repay you for all that you've done for me."

Zondra said, "Quit with all this mushy stuff, girl—I'm an aunt now, and I'm going to spoil my nephew rotten." I told her go ahead and be my guest; however, I didn't know how she was ever going to top the rock star welcome he'd received today from his grandparents. She indicated she had a few tricks up her on sleeve as well and she was full of surprises, reminding me of my recommitment ceremony in Jamaica. After cleaning up the kitchen, we left the room arm in arm headed to the patio to sit with the rest of the family.

CHAPTER 56

With so much commotion about SJ's adoption, I almost forgot that Diane was going to get married. I had to quickly turn my attention from being a first-time mother to assisting with her wedding. To say that Diane was nervous wouldn't even come close. I guess she was worried that David was going to pull another David Copperfield and disappear.

The good thing about this wedding was that Diane and David were planning it together, and she would only need for Deborah, Zondra, and me to assist with decorating the church. She insisted that her wedding was going to be simply lovely, without cameras or stars in attendance, because this time she was doing it with David. I expressed to her that was the way it was intended to be.

I was honored and surprised when Diane called me one night and said that she had a huge favor to ask of me. I asked, "What is it?"

"Would you allow Samuel James to be the ring bearer?"

"Of course."

Before she hung up the phone, she said, "Niecey, I'm proud of you. I know I can be impossible at times, but you and Deborah have supported me in everything I've done even when I've been a brat. I appreciate all of the sisterly advice you've offered me over the years. SJ is lucky to have you as a mom. I just hope that when my time comes around that I'm half the mother you and Deborah are to your children. I love you, sister."

Diane's words were comforting. I knew she was thick in the skull, but through it all it appeared she had listened to some of the things I'd said to her. I told my baby sister, "You're more than welcome. I love you too, but now I have one more job to do— get you down the aisle and married before David changes his mind again."

She said, "Not funny, Niecey," before she hung up the telephone.

Mom and Pops were excited about Diane's upcoming nuptials. My mom couldn't believe that this day was here—again. My husband and his brother constantly were calling David to make sure his head was in the right place and that he wasn't having second thoughts, again. Diane knew that they were badgering David and spoke with both of them, advising them that she and

David had had numerous conversations about their wedding. He'd backed out on her once, but if he had any plans on doing it again, she would guarantee he would spend the rest of his life looking over his shoulder because she was not going to be left at the altar a second time without someone suffering.

I told my husband that my sister was something else. She was going to get David down that aisle; whether she had to drag him or threaten his life, either way he was going to marry her. We laughed at the thought of Diane dragging David up to the altar kicking and screaming. I told Malachi to mind his own business and leave David and Diane alone, once they were married he would have plenty of opportunities to tease and torment them.

The wedding was quickly approaching; I asked Malachi if they were going to throw another bachelor party for David. Malachi said, "Hell no, Niecey—we gave that dude a party the first time, and look what he did. What we'll do is hire some bodyguards to stand by his room and make sure he doesn't sneak out in the middle of the night—but that's all he's getting from me." We laughed that David had ruined any chance of enjoying his last night as a bachelor and he was just going to have to do without the usual festivities.

CHAPTER 57

The wedding went off without a problem. SJ carried the rings down the aisle. Diane looked beautiful in her cream-colored strapless gown, while David was handsome in his white-and-cream tuxedo, but he was sweating bullets and I could understand why. That husband of mine and his bully of a brother must have frightened the poor man to death, which was why he stood up there looking like somebody about to be executed. Frightened or not, when it was time to recite the vows and exchange wedding rings, David seemed to have gotten all the jitters out, and he was confidant and sure of himself by the time he and Diane were introduced as husband and wife.

Everyone clapped for joy. We were all ready to celebrate because this was the last Martin girl to get married, and it was a joyous occasion. At the reception, you couldn't get Diane and David off of the dance floor. Dad had his dance with Diane with me, as Deborah and Zondra stood by with tears in our eyes. After the bouquet and garter belt had been thrown to the single people in the room, Diane and David said their good-byes and took off to the airport, en route to Aruba for their honeymoon. I was glad Diane had already left the building and was in the air because what happened next would have devastated her on her wedding day.

My parents were on the dance floor enjoying themselves when my mother yelled for Kevin to assist her in helping my father to his seat. My sister and I hurried to his side, and he tried to pretend that everything was fine. I didn't want to panic, but my dad didn't look well at all. I knew he had to be ill when he asked Kevin to call for help because his chest was hurting.

I'm sure it didn't take the ambulance that long to arrive, but to me it seemed like an eternity. My head was spinning and I felt like throwing up. Once Dad was loaded into the ambulance, the entire family followed to the hospital. Deborah and Kevin dropped the kids including SJ at their home before coming to the hospital themselves. When they joined us, we were all waiting in the visitors' area for an update on Daddy's condition.

I couldn't sit still, and I could feel Malachi watching me like a hawk. My stomach was doing somersaults and I had to sit down because the room kept spinning. I didn't want to have a panic attack, not now. Everyone was pacing back and forth.

It was close to three hours before a physician came out to talk to us. When he entered the room, we all stood and waited for his information. He said, "He's going to be fine. He had a mild heart attack, but he made it to the hospital just in time. We're going to keep him for the next few days to monitor his heart and make sure he's stable enough to resume his daily activities."

We were elated about the doctor's news regarding my dad's condition. Or at least I thought I was, but after the doctor left, the next thing I remember was Malachi hugging me before I hit the ground. When I came to, I was lying in a hospital bed with my family surrounding me. I said, "I'm sorry, ya'll. Shoot, I didn't mean to have another panic attack. I thought I had it under control."

Malachi responded, "Oh, it's OK. Baby—you have a good reason for fainting this time."

I told Malachi to stop fooling around. Then I noticed all of my family was looking at me with weird grins on their faces. I asked them, "What the heck is wrong with you all—and what's so funny?"

Zondra looked at Malachi and asked, "Should we all tell her together?"

Malachi said, "Yeah, on the count of three." He counted them off, then I heard them in unison shout, "*You're pregnant!*"

I looked at everyone standing there, Malachi, Zondra, Malcolm, Deborah, Kevin, and my mom, searching for a hint that they were joking with me. I didn't know what to say or how to act about the news. I stammered out, "How did that happen?"

Deborah said, "Well, if you don't know, we don't know either. All I know is that it wasn't immaculate conception."

Malachi was blushing and rubbing my stomach saying, "My baby is going to have a baby. This is some day. I can't wait to tell my folks."

Before he could say anything else, Malcolm said, "I guess this is the perfect end to today, except that I can't let my twin brother outshine me. Zondra and I have some news of our own. We were going to wait to tell everyone, that we're expecting also."

All the women began to scream and the nurses thought something terrible had happened so they raced to us to see what all the commotion was about. Kevin let them know that tonight had been one of blessings and good news. I looked at Zondra and asked, "Girl, how come you didn't say anything?"

She said, "We were planning for Diane's wedding and I didn't want to say anything until we got her married, but since you beat me to the punch, there goes the surprise. I had to swear Malcolm to secrecy—I thought he would just burst if he didn't tell someone, especially his brother."

"This was definitely some night," my mother commented. She was on her way upstairs to see my dad. They now had him in a room, and my mom was the only one permitted to visit him, they didn't want too many people bothering him in his delicate condition. Mom couldn't wait to see him so that she could share the good news with him.

It had seemed this night was headed for disaster with my dad suffering a heart attack, but God wasn't ready for him just yet, and I'm glad. I want him to be around to see my children grow up and be a constant in their lives just as he has been for me and my sisters.

His stay in the hospital wasn't that long and soon he was home resting and being an obedient patient. My mother wouldn't let him lift a finger to do anything except go to the bathroom. We all agreed that we wouldn't tell Diane and David about Dad's heart attack until they returned from their honeymoon. My parents didn't feel the need to alarm them, especially since my dad had been released from the hospital. There was no need for them to worry while they were so far away, and there was nothing they could have done anyway.

Now that everything was back to normal, I had a lot of planning to do in order to get ready for the arrival of our baby. Samuel James was elated that he was going to be a big brother. All he kept asking was, "Since I'm the big brother, my little sister or little brother has to listen to me, right?"

I told him, "Yes, they have to listen to you, but only if you are telling them the right things to do."

He said "Alright!"

It turned out that I was six weeks pregnant when I fainted in the hospital. I guess I'd been so busy planning for SJ and then Diane's wedding that I hadn't even realized I'd missed my period. Talk about crazy.

If that don't top things, my best friend Zondra was two months pregnant, and we could share this experience together. These Donahue men don't do anything half-assed. Now they were both walking around like proud peacocks because Zondra and I are pregnant at the same time. I keep telling Malachi that it was just a coincidence, but he said, "Coincidence my foot, girl—this is divine order. I got one son, now I've got another one on the way. I couldn't ask for anything else."

I had to quickly correct him and say, "Excuse me, Mr. Donahue, but who says that I'm carrying a boy? For all you know, this could be my precious daughter who will have you eating out of her hand. By the way, I'm not sure I want to know the sex of the baby beforehand—I want it to be a surprise."

Malachi said, "Woman, don't you know that Donahue men only make boys? And you should have had enough surprises by now, but if you don't want to know the sex of the baby until delivery, then I can wait also."

I jumped up and kissed him. "Thank you, sweetheart."

"Hey, cut out all that jumping around—you're going to make my baby sick." I smacked him on the back for trying to be funny.

Zondra had also decided to wait until her baby was born to learn the sex. She and I had to attend birthing classes together along with our husbands. It was fun having someone to share this experience with. However, the further along in our pregnancies we got, the more our husbands dreaded going to Lamaze class with us. We got a kick out of seeing these two big strong men become nauseous when they saw actual footage of childbirth.

Malcolm had the nerve to ask Zondra, "Do I really have to be in the delivery room with you?"

Zondra told him, "You were there when I conceived your child, and you're going to be there when I give birth."

I looked at Malachi and said, "Same thing goes for you." Zondra and I had to get our amusement somehow, and they made it easy for us to have something to laugh at.

What was not funny was that at six months, I was put on complete bed rest. The doctor said that my blood pressure was extremely high and since I had already lost a baby before under traumatic conditions, I was a high-risk pregnancy. I was jealous because Zondra didn't seem to have near as much trouble with her pregnancy as I was having. She was able to continue working and she exercised, which is why she didn't look like a whale unlike me. My mother-in-law came over to the house to make sure I was alright throughout the day, and she was a big help with SJ, making sure he did his homework. I managed to read him bedtime stories and make sure he got a hot breakfast before he went to school every morning. That was the most exertion that my husband would allow me, because he wanted to make sure I was following the doctor's orders and staying in bed.

By my eighth month of sitting in bed watching every Court TV program, I was sick. I was turning into a Judge Mathis, Judge Joe Brown, *People's Court*, Judge Judy junkie. Plus, I couldn't see my feet any more, and I just wanted labor and delivery to be over with.

With one more month to go, Malachi tried to amuse me the best way that he could. We had family night down in his theater room, or sometimes he and SJ sat in the bed with me and watched television, SJ would always fall asleep and Malachi would carry him to his room. I would just sit and marvel at the fact that SJ had come into our family; it felt as if he'd been a part of our lives forever.

When I thought about all of the nights I'd spent crying over the loss of my first child, I was comforted by these words from Psalm 30:6: "Weeping may endure for a night, but joy comes in the morning." God knows our heart's desires, and he'd seen fit for Samuel James to enter our lives, then he blessed us again with this pregnancy. I could now relate to Tabitha Patterson and I could share this testimony with any individual who felt their prayers were not being answered. I was living proof that all you have to do is wait on the Lord.

CHAPTER 58

My due date was swiftly approaching, and Zondra was expected to deliver any day now. She was two day past her due date, and the doctor said he was going to induce labor because there was no need to prolong the inevitable. Zondra would have delivered her baby herself if she knew how, but this pregnancy was making her nervous because she wasn't sure she would make a good mother. I had to remind her that she managed to take care of her little brother and sister after her parents passed away, all while maintaining her grades and track scholarship, so delivering this baby should be no problem. Zondra relaxed after I told her that she would go into the hospital tomorrow, and by the end of the day have a new addition to the family, so she needed to quit with all of her worrying.

After I ended my call to Zondra, Malachi lay in bed next to me and rubbed my belly. He spoke to his unborn child, "Hey little buddy, or little girl, I'm your daddy. You have the prettiest mother in the whole wide world. I want you to know that we've waited for you for a long time, and I'm excited about your arrival. I also want you to know that we are going to have so much fun together. You have a big brother who can't wait to teach you how to throw and catch a football."

I said, "Hey, my daughter doesn't want to be taught how to play football."

"Well, in that case your big brother can't wait until you start cheering for his football team." He looked at me and asked, "Was that better?"

"Very funny, Mr. Donahue."

Before we drifted off to sleep, Malachi asked me, "Honey, do you remember when I told you that you were going to have all of my babies?"

I said, "Yes, I do, and this is just the beginning of many more. But you have to love me no matter how big and fat I get."

"It's just more of you to love, baby doll."

"I love you, Malachi Alan Donahue."

"Back at cha."

It was six o'clock in the morning when our telephone rang and Malcolm told us that he and Zondra were at the hospital because she had just gone into labor. He told us there was no need to rush, the doctor said it would be quite some time before she was ready for delivery, and he would just let the baby predict the arrival time. I told Malachi I wasn't going to miss this experience for anything and I anxiously got ready to join Zondra at the hospital.

After we were dressed and packed things for SJ, we dropped him off at my in-laws home, then headed to the hospital to be with Malcolm and Zondra. It was a good thing we arrived when we did because Malcolm looked as if he were going to pass out. He couldn't stand the sight of Zondra being in pain. I took over, rubbing her back when the contractions started and feeding her ice chips. Malcolm and I alternated with the soothing techniques, and when the doctor arrived, he said that it wouldn't be long before Zondra was ready to deliver, then he took one look at me and asked, "When are you due?"

"In a few weeks."

"Not by the look of your pants." We all looked down to see a big wet spot in the middle of my crotch.

"What do I do?" I asked.

The doctor said, "Nurse, admit this woman and prep her for delivery as well."

I told them, "I'm not ready, besides Zondra needs me."

The nurse said, "There's enough room in here for both of you. You can have the bed next to your friend." Malachi and Malcolm were just staring at one another, unsure of what to do next.

When the nurse examined me, she told the doctor that I must have been in labor for quite some time because I was fully dilated. Now I know that I had been through my Lamaze classes, but to hear her actually say that to me made me forget everything I'd been taught over the past two months. I drew a blank and couldn't remember a thing.

Malachi got his scrubs on and said, "Baby, we got this. Besides, it's only right that we have our baby first—I always beat Malcolm at everything."

I looked at him and said, "What are you talking about, man? A human being is about to come through my vagina and you're talking about beating Malcolm."

"You're right—I was just joking."

Just then a fierce pain came from my back all the way down to my toes making me cry out. The nurse said, "Darling, you're too far along, and we can't administer any pain medication." God knows if I wasn't saved, at that precise moment I would have thought of some word combinations that would've made her head spin. I've never felt any pain like this before in my life, and all I wanted to do was pass out and wake up when it was all over.

Meanwhile, Zondra was sitting next to me, without a grimace on her face. I guess her epidural was kicking in now. I couldn't think because this pain was so intense. I told Malachi, "Baby, I'm going to die if I don't get any pain medicine." He kept trying to urge me to use my breathing techniques, but I yelled at him, "It hurts to breathe!"

The nurse added her two cents in: "Darling, young girls have babies every day. You'll be just fine once it's all over."

I said, "Lady, please shut up—I don't want to hear that mess. All I want is some drugs to make this pain go away." I could hear Zondra and Malcolm laughing from behind the curtain. If I'd been near either one of them, I think I would've punched them.

Malachi said, "Stop being rude, Niecey."

I told him, "I couldn't help it—it wasn't me talking, it was the pain."

The doctor came over. "I see the baby's head crowning, so it's time to push." They positioned my legs and Malachi turned into a birthing coach, giving me instructions on when to push. There were so many people in the room because of Zondra and me both being in labor, but at that moment I didn't care who was getting a sneak preview of my goodies as all I wanted was for that child to come out.

I think I gave four good pushes, then I heard the doctor say, "We have baby girl number one." Then the doctor said, "Give me another push. This time all it took was two pushes and the baby was out. He said, "We have baby girl number two."

The nurses took the girls to make sure they were fine while Malachi stood next to me looking bewildered. I said, "Well, there you go Mr. Donahue—you doubled your pleasure. Looks like Donahue men are capable of making some little girls, huh?"

The doctor had enough time to remove his scrubs and change before Zondra began her delivery. I didn't want to miss anything with the birth of her child. Even though I couldn't move, I was all ears. I didn't even hear Zondra scream in pain when the doctor was saying that we had a baby boy. I could hear Malcolm say, "I knew it."

Then the doctor shocked us all when he said, "I don't believe it."

Malcolm sounded worried as he said, "What's the problem, doc?"

"It's another baby!"

In unison, Malachi, Malcolm, and I cried, "What?"

CHAPTER 59

It had been three months since we were doubly blessed with the arrival of all of the children. Misty Faith Donahue and Morgan Hope Donahue were twenty minutes older than their twin cousins, Matthew Logan Donahue and Michael Lucas Donahue. All the children were healthy, and they were indeed a handful. My parents came to Atlanta to assist me with the twins and SJ until I recuperated, and my mother-in-law and one of Zondra's aunts helped her during her recovery. Zondra and I had never disclosed to anyone that we were carrying twins, we both wanted to surprise our husbands and each other apparently. We were still in awe of our new arrivals, now I had my son and daughters to be thankful for. At this moment, it seemed my life couldn't get any better.

SJ was being the proud big brother. He had two sisters to protect, and he was affectionate and protective of them as soon as they came home from the hospital. My dad was feeling better and I was glad he had enough strength to come and visit. I was able to rest knowing that my mom was taking care of things for me around the house. I tried to keep up with SJ and these twins who played tag team when they started crying, I'm suddenly in awe of my mom, because I don't know how she managed to raise me and my sisters without going insane. I asked my Mom how she did it, she replied, "There were plenty of days that I wanted to run for the door, unlike you, I didn't have anyone to depend on and help me out, and men didn't take part in rearing children like they do today. I'm glad that I can help you out, and you're lucky to have a man like Malachi."

I told her, "Yeah, I know—he's been staring at the girls every night when I put them down after their feeding. They already have him wrapped around their little fingers, and it's adorable to see how he interacts with them.

My sisters had been spoiling the babies since their arrival. When they came up to see the babies after I was discharged from the hospital, they managed to buy so many toys, clothes, and latest baby invention that I was set for the next year. Diane was extremely helpful with the girls and took a keen interest in watching me bathe and change diapers.

While she was watching me nurse the babies one evening, I asked her if she was thinking about starting a family with David anytime soon. She responded, "Not after watching how these girls latch onto your titties and suck on them like they're cow udders. No, thank you—I'm in no hurry." We laughed, but nursing the girls made me feel as if I shared a bond with them. I loved to look down at their faces and have them stare back at me. I fell in love all over again with each feeding.

Once when Malachi watched me feed the girls, he said, "I never thought I would see the day when I had to share your breasts with anyone else. But I'll move over for my girls anytime." Motherhood is the best feeling in the world. I had the opportunity to carry these little beings, and I was privileged to bring forth new life. Now I was responsible for raising them to be moral and honest individuals. I prayed that I would do a good job with each of them. The sky was the limit as far as their future was concerned. I would equip them with the tools they needed in order to survive in this world, but it was going to definitely be up to them to make wise choices as they grew up.

When I expressed my fears and concerns about the girls to my mom, she told me, "You're just like every first time mother. I wanted to protect you girls from everything that was harmful in this world, but if I did that, then you wouldn't be as strong as you are today. Niecey, you will make mistakes—Lord knows that I have—but as long as you bring them up to fear God, teach them how to respect themselves and others, remain firm with your decisions with them, and work with Malachi as a team when you discipline them, then you will be alright. I'm not saying there won't be tough times. Lord knows you girls added to the grey hairs on my head, and during your teenage years, I just wanted to lock you all up until your hormones settled down. But for now just stop worrying about how these kids will turn out. You and Malachi are good examples as parents, and their grandparents are willing to spoil them when you two get too hard on them."

I thanked my mom for her advice and told her, "If I'm half the mom to the kids that you've been to me, they will be perfect." We hugged each other and shared a moment that only mothers could understand.

Things over at Zondra and Malcolm's house were just as thrilling. Zondra called and expressed to me that she was so in love with the boys that she didn't know if she could stand being away from them once her maternity leave was over. She also wasn't sure she wanted them to be placed in child care after hearing so many horrible stories about child abuse and neglect, she wanted to make sure they were going to be given the love and attention they needed in the early stages of their lives.

I told her that they had a stay-at-home auntie who would love nothing more than to watch over them while their parents were at work. Zondra was skeptical regarding my suggestion, she wondered how I would have enough strength or mental capacity to handle four babies and an eight-year-old boy on a daily basis. I told her "Fine—just take them over to a stranger's house so you can sit in your office all day long and wonder if the boys are being fed or sitting around in dirty diapers. You can also think about all of the money you will be wasting sending two babies to child care instead of being at ease knowing they are in the comfort of a loving home with a responsible adult while they bond with their cousins and have a grand old time."

Zondra saw things a little differently after I painted that picture for her. She wanted to talk things over with Malcolm and see how flexible her employer could be. She was going to suggest working half days at the office and doing most of her work at home where she could be with the boys more. I told her that sounded like a good idea. "Just think of all the business you've generated for that law firm—they would be crazy not to entertain the concept to keep their most loyal and dedicated employee." Zondra liked the pep talk I gave her, and even though her intuition told her that her bosses wouldn't take too kindly to her suggestion, she had to try.

Zondra told me later, that day when Malcolm came home from work, he found her in a foul mood. She was ranting and raving about how she couldn't believe the people down at Schwartz & Simon, LLP, where she had been employed for the past ten years had the nerve to treat her like a peasant when she asked if she could have an alternate work schedule that would allow her to work from home, coming into the office when she had to meet with clients or negotiate their contracts. Her bosses advised her that they were sorry but they just couldn't run the risk of everyone in the office seeking preferential treatment just because they had a baby. Zondra calmed down long enough to explain the entire story to Malcolm as to why she was livid. She told him that she loved being an attorney, and it was something she knew she was good at, but being a mother had changed her priorities. However, she thought she could do both without feeling as if she was being neglectful to either.

As usual, Malcolm had tried to soothe her by standing behind her and massaging her shoulders. She told me that when she felt Malcolm's touch, the tension escaped from her body, and she said, "Thank you, Malcolm—I'm just frustrated. I'm sorry for going on like a lunatic."

Malcolm said, "That's what I'm here for, sugar. I know that you're a damn good attorney, Z, and your bosses are shortsighted for not taking your request into consideration, especially since you've brought some big name entertainers and athletes to that firm and generated oodles of money for them. Zondra, you've been in the business long enough, and you have an impeccable reputation for going above and beyond the call of duty for the individuals you represent. You should honestly think about starting your own law firm. You could work out of the office here at the house until we find you a suitable space elsewhere."

Zondra smiled at him and said, "You know what? Not only have you been blessed with good looks, but there's a brain inside of that head of yours. Do you really mean what you said about me working out of the home?"

"Yes."

"Well then, on Monday morning I'm going to march myself right into Schwartz & Simon and turn in my resignation. I'll also let them know that Donahue & Associates will be an agency to reckon with. They have let the wrong woman loose, now they better watch their backs."

"That's my girl, give them hell, but who are these associates?"

"I don't know yet as I haven't figured that much out, but it sounds good." Then she said they both laughed as they went into the nursery to check on Matthew and Michael.

CHAPTER 60

The law firm of Donahue & Associates quickly blossomed into a big business. Once Zondra's clients received notice that she was no longer with Schwartz & Simon, they all jumped ship along with her. Two of the younger lawyers and a clerk followed Zondra as well so she didn't have to worry about who her "associates" would be for too long. She didn't even have to work out of her home either, with the revenue from the clients who came with her; Zondra was able to rent a spacious downtown office. She even had enough room to create a nursery there for the twins, that way she could devote her attention to her family and job without feeling as if she were slighting either.

It wasn't unusual for Malcolm to drop in during lunchtime and take Zondra and the boys out if her schedule permitted, being in real estate allowed him the flexibility to help Zondra while also bonding with the boys. I even agreed to work part-time as Zondra's secretary; it provided me an opportunity to get out of the house with Misty and Morgan for a few hours. Having adult contact was refreshing, and I was glad to help my friend in any way that I could. I bet those guys over at Zondra's old law firm were regretting that they didn't take her up on her offer. This undoubtedly, had turned out to be a good professional leap for her, one she should have taken a lot sooner.

CHAPTER 61

This weekend, Samuel James will be celebrating his tenth birthday, and we promised to throw him a party he would never forget. He was excited and took the liberty of writing down all of the toys and video games that he would like to have. He was the first grandchild, and his grandparents indulged his every request. Malachi and I hosted the grand event to which we invited all of SJ's classmates along with our family. Our son wanted a pool party, so I had to make sure there was enough adult supervision because I didn't want anyone's child to drown at my home.

Malachi was the master chef on the grill, and he wouldn't let me taste test anything, no matter how much I tried to persuade him with my sultry gazes. All he said was, "Keep it up and I'm gonna put this spatula down and take you in the house and make another set of twins." I hurriedly found something else to do. Both sets of twins were walking now, and having four toddlers running around kept us all on our toes, so the thought of any more at this moment wasn't even funny.

My sisters and parents made it to town for the occasion. Diane and David were as happy as ever. LMS was thriving, and she mentioned to me that she and David were thinking of relocating to the area and opening another boutique since Atlanta had become a mecca for young black entrepreneurs. I reminded her she wasn't young, and although she and David might be making a smart move by branching out, she should be thinking about starting a family instead of believing money can buy everything.

Diane asked, "Why? I can live vicariously through you, Deborah, and Zondra. I don't have to have a bunch of screaming kids to know my worth as a woman, David and I are enjoying each other's company, and I love the life I'm living right now."

"I'm not saying that having children makes your life complete, Diane, but it's just the greatest feeling in the world as a woman, and I know that David would love to plant his seed and watch it grow."

Diane's response was vulgar, just as I suspected it would be: "Oh for your information, David has been planting plenty of seeds—they just haven't been fertilized since I'm still on the Pill." I just shook my head at that girl and left her sitting next to the pool by herself; she's still so simple.

It seemed Diane wasn't the only one having ideas of leaving the Sunshine State. Now that my parents were retired, they realized they were tired of the escalating crime and high traffic in Miami, plus the cost of living was escalating. They mentioned to me that they were thinking about selling the house and moving to Atlanta. I thought it was a good idea, and I also knew that as Diane was making plans to relocate, it wouldn't be too long before Deborah jumped on the bandwagon, there was no way she was going to be left behind in Miami. All she had to do was persuade Kevin to request a transfer and because Kevin could never say no to Deborah, so it looks like the entire Martin clan will be moving to Georgia.

When they heard my family was making preparations to relocate to Miami, Malachi's parents offered their help in finding homes in our area. I told Malachi, "Look baby, I love my family, but you make sure your parents show them some homes that would mean a considerable amount of travel time for them to visit us."

Malachi laughed. "Woman, we think too much alike. I already pulled the listings for properties within a forty-mile radius. I will have them spread all across Atlanta so there will be no surprise visits."

I told Malachi, "I knew that I married you for a good reason."

"Yes, and if I remember correctly that reason had you screaming and crying on our first night together."

"Uh, it's been so long ago and my mind is slipping with old age. I think that you're going to have to remind me of what you are talking about."

With a smirk on his face, Malachi asked, "Are the kids asleep?"

"Indeed they are."

Malachi picked me up and carried me to the bedroom. At the doorway I said, "Oh, now it's all coming back to me."

CHAPTER 62

Having my family here has been a blessing in disguise. I received my interior decorating license all while depending on the help of my parents and sisters to assist with the kids when I needed them to. Diane did open another boutique, and LMS Creations II proved to be a very smart move. She learned how to monitor the merchandise, profits, and employees via computer so she didn't have to make frequent trips to Miami to oversee the everyday operations of the original store.

Deborah also started a chain for her Deb's Doo Right Hair Salon; one of her trusted beauticians stepped up to manage the salon in Miami while Deborah found a suitable location in Atlanta and built up her clientele there. Finding females in Atlanta willing to pay top price for beauty wasn't hard. Deb could still work a hot comb and some curlers, and most of her clients were the wives or girlfriends of the athletes and entertainers Zondra represented. Once Deb hooked up their hair, they could always find an interesting outfit at LMS Creations II to complete their look of sophistication for a party or gala. Zondra knew how to network and she even dropped my name to her clients if they were interested in decorating their newly purchased homes, which undoubtedly was sold to them by someone in the P&M Donahue real estate company. This was a family affair, and everyone was in on the act.

To bring back tradition, we started having Sunday dinner at my parents' home after church. The crowd had grown, but the entertainment remained the same. We could always count on Diane to say something crude, which got Malcolm and Malachi started on David and how he should handle his woman, then Kevin and Deborah would chime in on their ideas for peace and harmony. My in-laws and parents just looked at all of us around the table as we argued, cracked jokes at one another, and professed our love for our mate. My dad and mom held hands and smiled approvingly at one another.

Once my father-in-law asked my parents, "Is this what you all were missing down in Miami that made you decide to move to Atlanta?"

In unison my parents replied, "Yeah."

EPILOGUE

It's been eight years since Samuel James came into our lives. I would have never thought I could love him as much as I do. As I look back on all the years, I wonder how his life would have turned out if Rebecca had lived and been a part of his life, but I guess I'll never know. I just hope that wherever she's spending eternity, she can look at SJ and be proud of the man he's becoming. Everything that is good in him came from the love that Malachi and I showered on him, and I don't see a trace of Rebecca Bennett in him.

She was laid to rest a long time ago, and now the memories of her actions no longer haunt me. I've made peace with the past, and I've forgiven all that she did. If it weren't for her, I wouldn't have found a man like Malachi who is a definitely a godsend. He's a man of his word, and he has kept his promise to make me the happiest woman in the world. My husband and the father of my children is the glue that holds this family together. He has been all that God has called him to be: the head of this family, protector, and provider. My love for him grows stronger with each passing day.

As I sit here watching Malachi play basketball with SJ, I remember something Zondra said to me when we adopted him, "He looks just like you two." Anyone comparing him to Misty and Morgan cheering on the sidelines couldn't really tell that SJ isn't our biological son. I would die for him just as I would for my other children. SJ will be graduating from high school in a year. He's turned into quite the track star, and he's being heavily recruited by some of the top schools in the country. Whatever decision he makes, I'll be there to support him, but I selfishly wish that he remains close to home (that's the protective mother in me). All of my children are turning out to be the joy of our lives, and I love creating special moments that they will remember just as my parents did for me.

I just wish my dad were here to see the children grow up. He suffered a severe heart attack two years ago, and his absence has left a hole in this family. I miss him terribly. My mom is coping with his death by immersing herself in church activities and spending time with her grandchildren.

My sisters' invasion of Atlanta was successful, and they've now become household names. Deborah only has select clients and her schedule is no longer overbooked. Her sons are now in college and the baby, Diamond, will be entering middle school in the fall. Ms. Diane finally slowed down long enough for David to fertilize her eggs and they have a two-year-old daughter named Devine who is the spitting image of Diane. Lord, I don't think the world is ready for another Diane.

My beloved friend Zondra has added two more attorneys to her office, and she is pregnant with her and Malcolm's daughter. Malcolm couldn't be happier; he's working side by side with his brother, and even after all of this time the two of them are still thick as thieves.

I am blessed to have this family, and I always pray that God extends his arm of protection around them all and keeps us safe. When I think about all that has transpired over the years, I know my Heavenly Father had a plan for me. He kept me safe and secure and as Psalm 13:5–6 says, "I trust in your unfailing love, I will rejoice because you have rescued me. I will sing to the Lord because he has been so good to me,"